The blond slipped out of the elevator just as the doors closed and stood staring again, obviously enjoying Sarah's discomfiture. Sarah finally turned and began the long walk to her door. The blond fell into step behind her.

My God, Sarah thought. I'm being stalked. Her head swam a little and she realized that it had been a long time since she had felt this way in the presence of another woman. She wouldn't let herself think that this was the beginning of something meaningful, that this was the moment, the first glance that meant romance and a life of forever afters. This was not anything like that. It was lust, pure and simple, and well, why not enjoy it?

EMBRACE IN MOTION

by

Karin Kallmaker

Bella
BOOKS

2003

Bella Books, Inc.
P.O. Box 10543
Tallahassee, FL 32302

First published 1997 by Naiad Press

Printed in the United States of America on acid-free paper
First Edition

Editor: Christine Cassidy
Cover designer: Bonnie Liss (Phoenix Graphics)

ISBN 1-931513-39-2

For Maria, who taught me the meaning of romance
And Kelson, who taught me a new kind of love

The Seventh is Up, Up and Away

Melissa

EMBRACE (èm-brâs′)
[Middle English *embracen*, from Old French
embracer] embrace (verb); embraced,
embracing, embraces (verb, transitive);
embrace (noun)
1. To clasp with the arms, usually as an
   expression of affection; to hug; to pull
   close.
2. To take up willingly or eagerly accept.
3. To enclose; encircle; engulf.
4. To twine around.

1

*She had been forced into prudence in her youth,
she learned romance as she grew older. (Jane
Austen)*

The man who set his half-empty glass on the bar
was attractive and he had a definite swagger in his
manner. Sarah began to give him her best "hands
off" look, then realized he was familiar. The memory
clicked — they'd met at a workshop during last year's
convention.

"So, hey, sweet thing, got any plans for dinner
and breakfast?" He smirked and his charming blue
eyes actually twinkled.

Sarah decided to reply in kind. She slid her hand
along his thigh, making him jump. "Hey, lover, buy a
lady a drink."

Geoff burst out laughing and leaned comfortably

against the bar. "I'd almost think you'd had practice picking up men in bars."

"Never men, as you well know. I noticed that the diversity training session this year doesn't mention the unmentionable again."

"Me, too. I guess our comments on the evaluation form last year didn't open any eyes." Geoff took a sip from his glass, grimaced and settled on the bar stool next to her.

"I signed up again," Sarah said. "The session is tomorrow and I'm going to bring it up if I can keep up my nerve."

"Lucky you," Geoff said, "working for CompuSoft where you can be out."

"You're still at — what was it, H and G Chemical?"

"Yes, but I have a cunning plan," he said with one of his heartbreaking smiles. "They've fired at least two research guys I know were gay and neither of them made a fuss. But if they find out about me I'll be a client for Lambda Legal so fast, it'll make their head spin. I'll be sitting pretty."

"After a long legal battle," Sarah said practically. "Are you serious?"

"No," he said. "I mean yes, I'll sue if they fire me, but I don't really want to. I don't suppose there are any more openings for patent attorneys at CompuSoft? I'd be willing to relocate." Geoff mimed a begging dog and panted.

"Down, boy! I've got a waiting list a mile long of people who would be willing to pay me large sums of money just to put in a good word for them."

"So I'm stuck writing patents for the latest cleaning fluid in a company where being a single man makes you suspect. Actually, that was why I sauntered over here." His eyes were twinkling again.

4

"Did you know you have Robert Redford's eyes?" She had a feeling that it wasn't news to him.

He gave her an annoyed look. "So I've been told. I have to tell you it's one of the reasons I like hanging out with gay girls. I get tired of being hit on." He brushed back his crisp, blond hair in a gesture at once unconscious and decidedly attractive.

"Sorry I said something so cruel, you poor beleaguered man," Sarah said dryly. If ever there had been a man who was her type, Geoff was it. Exactly the looks for armor and a white charger. He'd look really good in a jerkin and tights.

Geoff laughed. "Anyway, I came over here because the butthead of a co-worker at the table with me keeps trying to trick me into admitting I'm gay — you know the type. He mentions show tunes and Judy Garland like I'm going to squeal and launch into 'Somewhere Over the Rainbow.' " He shook his head with a sigh and sipped his drink.

"So," Sarah prodded, "how did Mr. Butthead make you come over here?"

"He's stupid enough to bet me a hundred bucks that I can't get a woman to dance with me. He apparently believes that women have built-in radar and know I'm gay and therefore . . ."

"Therefore won't dance with you? He's certifiable. A woman who likes to dance would dance with Bigfoot if he knew how to fox-trot." Sarah casually surveyed the room in order to sneak a glance at Mr. Butthead, who was busy leering at the cocktail waitress. He was a pasty bit of pudding — his palms were probably perpetually damp.

"I said he's an idiot. So how would you like to split the hundred with me?" He gestured at the dance floor. The song had just changed from a raucous and unintelligible disco song to Bonnie

5

Raitt's sultry "Let's Give Them Something to Talk About."

"Perfect timing," Sarah said and she let Geoff spin her out onto the sparsely coupled dance floor.

She loved to dance and hadn't been dancing since the break-up with Ellen. She hadn't thought that there'd be any chance to dance at the annual patent attorney's convention. When you don't generally dance with men, and know no other lesbians in the association, you don't need your dancing shoes. Then again, when she'd arrived and seen on the conference board that there was a lesbian writer's conference sharing space in the hotel, she'd had a passing romantic fancy that she would meet someone and have a torrid fling that included dancing all night and walking with their pantlegs rolled up through the surf — a Hallmark moment — even though she knew perfectly well that there were no beaches with surf within 1,500 miles of Louisville, Kentucky.

The last thing she had dreamed she would do was dance with a man. And she'd certainly never dreamed she'd be dancing with a man as good as Geoff was proving to be. She sent the usual fond mental thank-you to Jenny, a champion ballroom dancer. The past had its good moments, yes indeed. Too bad the future looked so dull.

He drew her close during the refrain and said, "Here — I'll do you a favor." He led her smoothly to the opposite side of the dance floor and then slowly turned her so that she was looking over his shoulder at a table occupied only by women.

It was just a guess, but she was pretty sure they weren't patent attorneys. Far too much color and style in their attire and a hint of attitude in the brown suede and black leather bomber jackets on the backs of the chairs. Definitely from the writer's conference, and two of them were practically in each other's laps. She noticed that several of the men nearby couldn't take their eyes off of the lovebirds, including Mr. Butthead — the worm.

She made eye contact with a pale, anorexic brunette who responded with a pointed, disdainful glance at Sarah's high heels. Amused, Sarah snuggled closer to Geoff and then winked at the brunette. The brunette leaned over to the plump chocolate-skinned woman on her right and said something that Sarah guessed was probably uncomplimentary about straight women who flirted with lesbians.

She could feel Geoff laughing. "What *are* you doing?"

"Flirting," Sarah said. "Looking for Ms. Goodbar."

"I would have sworn you weren't that type of girl."

"I'm not, usually. But I'm not getting any younger and the nights are getting colder. Know what I mean?"

Geoff swung her into a flip out and they turned so Geoff was facing the table. He said into her ear, "I know what you mean. Well, there's a cute girl giving me death looks. Blond, but not a natural, I'd say."

"That's catty."

"Truthful."

"Let me see."

He turned her and then drew her to him for a cheek-to-cheek.

She regarded the blond woman through her lashes. *Cute* was not at all right, she thought. Striking, maybe, but neither cute nor beautiful. She would have to spend some time finding the right word for her. "Oo-la-la," Sarah said in Geoff's ear. "Maybe I should rent the U-Haul now."

7

Geoff laughed. "You women," he said with mock scathing. "Just go upstairs and have fun. It doesn't have to be forever after."

Ha, Sarah thought. She knew lots of women who would do just that, but she wasn't one of them. Never had been. It was her curse that she wanted more than what her friend Debra called "hello — let's fuck — so long" relationships. She had been so sure she'd hit the center of the happily-ever-after target with Ellen, but it had ended with broken bowstrings for both of them.

"I'd almost do it, but there's no one who suits me." Except the blond woman. Curly, shoulder-length blond hair. Long neck. Strong shoulders, but not too broad. But Sarah couldn't just walk over and ask her to dance. She just didn't feel up to braving the hostile stares as she approached, nor the hostile stares they were sure to get if they danced.

The song ended and Geoff led her back to the bar. "I'm going to collect my hundred, and then how about we split a bottle of expensive wine and room service delicacies and bitch about our love lives?"

"And going to my room with me is that much more cover for you, isn't it?" Sarah was teasing, but Geoff winced.

"I hadn't thought of it that way. But you're right."

"It's okay," Sarah said, putting her hand on his arm. "Go get Mr. Butthead's money, sir."

While she waited for Geoff, she glanced over at the table of women again and discovered the blond woman staring at her. Sarah fought down a blush as the other woman's expressive lips conveyed a flirtatious suggestion as she glanced at Geoff, then back at Sarah. Then with a tiny lift of one eyebrow

8

she promised Sarah anything Geoff could do and more.

Sarah gave way to the blush and was smiling involuntarily as Geoff returned. She felt positively devilish as she took Geoff's arm and sent the blond a parted-lip, come-and-get-me smile Sarah hoped she'd remember in her dreams.

The following morning Sarah had a thick head and sincerely hoped Geoff did too. They'd finished an impressive cabernet sauvignon and a platter of hors d'oeuvres, complained about women and men and the death of romance, railed against homophobia, then sighed together during the local late movie: *Camille*. Geoff had imitated Garbo's cough to perfection. It had been a fun evening, but far too much wine for her head. Now she was paying for it. If it hadn't been for the diversity session first thing she would have stayed in bed until lunch.

Last year she'd been glad to see the stodgy Association of American Patent Attorneys include a session on handling diversity in the workplace. CompuSoft had been having in-house sessions like it for years and although Sarah found them hokey at times, they were necessary. It took those sessions *and* a vocal and unwavering commitment to diversity on the part of all levels of upper management to make a place as open to work at as CompuSoft. It wasn't perfect, but at least in the legal department your private life didn't influence your work ratings.

They had been about halfway through last year's session when she'd muttered something about sexual diversity under her breath and the man sitting in front of her — one of the few white men in the room — had turned around and smiled. At the first opportunity to pair off, Geoff had joined her. They used the exercise time to discuss if they should make an issue of it and Geoff had almost gone along, but then he'd described the hostile atmosphere at H&G Chemical and they'd both realized he wasn't ready to put his job at risk. But on their evaluation forms, which were anonymous, they'd plainly and persuasively pointed out that diversity training was worthless when it wasn't diverse.

She also knew that if the training were to have any effect at all, it took someone gay to speak up. So as the Association's conference representative introduced the trainer, Sarah glanced through the materials and found that once again no mention was made of gays, lesbians or bisexuals. In fact, the only diversity the Association wanted to discuss was racial. They didn't even mention gender.

She glanced around the room. It seemed as if all of the people of color attending the conference were in the room. A session devoted to only race relations seemed to her a little bit like preaching to the choir. Women far outnumbered men, and their perspective wasn't going to be addressed at all. Geoff was nowhere in sight, the layabout, and if anyone else in the room was gay they were just as invisible as she was in her suit and heels.

She sighed, feeling cross. Anna Ramos, the Association's representative, introduced the bubbly and bright-eyed facilitator, who enthusiastically launched into a review of the goals of the session. When she paused to ask if everyone was comfortable with the agenda, Sarah raised her hand. The facilitator told Sarah to go right ahead with her comments.

"I would like to see the agenda expanded to cover more territory," Sarah said. "If we're going to talk about diversity, in addition to race I'd like to talk about dealing with the differing perceptions of men and women in the workplace." She took a deep breath. "And I'd like to have a dialog about making the workplace a safe place to be gay or lesbian or bisexual."

The facilitator's expression froze for a moment, then she gave Anna Ramos what could only be an "I told you so" look. Great, Sarah thought, the facilitator has experience with the subjects and obviously thinks it should be included.

"Would anyone like to comment on — Sarah, is it? — Sarah's suggestion to expand the agenda?"

Anna Ramos, the only woman of color on the Association's board, actually looked relieved. "I'd certainly be willing," she said, firmly. Sarah put two and two together. Anna had wanted the topics on the agenda but had been overruled by the Association committee which planned the conference.

A corpulent white man in the front of the room got to his feet with the air of a man taking charge of a situation. Here it comes, Sarah thought. Buck Thurgood was also on the AAPA board and Sarah suspected the only reason he was here was to keep an eye on Anna Ramos, who was, as everyone knew, a troublemaker with radical ideas that might lead to — horror of horrors — change.

"I'm not sure that our time limit will allow us to go so far afield," Buck said.

The facilitator said hastily, "We can fold these topics into the existing exercises with very little impact on our schedule."

"Well, I'm sure you think so," Thurgood said with a patronizing chuckle that made Sara see red. He

11

looked across the room to where Sarah still stood and said coolly, "Far be it for me to ignore a member's concern, but I wouldn't want to mire our worthwhile activity here with controversial topics."

"Diversity is controversial," a black man said from the middle of the room. He stood briefly to add, "If it weren't we wouldn't be here. I *would* like to talk about making peace between the sexes. I'm tired of taking the rap for the acts of other men and I guess I'd like to know why so many women I work with are angry."

The facilitator quickly said, "I hear a willingness to talk about gender in addition to race." She gave Buck a look that wasn't defiant, but rather suggested that he bow to the inevitable.

A petite Asian woman stood and said earnestly, "I think we're all fooling ourselves if we think we can ignore gays. I had this really great guy working for me and all of a sudden his performance drops to nothing. I tried to find out if he had some sort of personal problem, but he said no. Then I found out from someone else that his partner had left him. After that I knew how to work with him — just like when someone gets a divorce. I gave him time and space — helped him focus day-to-day for a while. But if I hadn't known what was up, I'd have fired him and lost one of my best people. After I told him he could be open about his private life with me, he admitted that he thought I was a homophobe because I'm Chinese . . . so we have to talk about all types of diversity because they're all interrelated. We need to end ignorance."

"I don't think we should talk about sex on the job," an older Asian man said.

Sarah, who was still standing, sighed. "If you tell me you and your girlfriend went to the movies

Saturday night, is that telling me about your sex life? So why can't I tell you that I went to the movies on Saturday with *my* girlfriend?"

The facilitator said smoothly, "It's clear we do have something to talk about and there's a lot of interest in this subject. It will be a simple matter to include these new topics in our discussion. Thank you, everyone, for being willing to speak your mind."

Sarah sat down and glanced at Buck. He looked as if he had spit up in his mouth, but his sour expression didn't diminish her satisfaction one iota. She smiled to herself and realized her headache was gone.

At the end of the day, Sarah paused in front of the guest room elevators. She was tempted to spend the night in her room with the Kay Scarpetta mystery she'd begun on the plane, but she wasn't in the mood for a thriller. She wandered into the hotel gift shop and found, to her delight, a paperback copy of *Pride and Prejudice*, an old favorite. An evening with Elizabeth Bennett, Fitzwilliam Darcy and subtle, understated romance would be delightful and more enjoyable than her convention option, which was joining the excursion to Churchill Downs. She was not going to go out into a 95-degree Louisville evening with 100% humidity. Besides, she'd been there before, on Derby Day, in the company of an elegant woman who had collected athlete lovers much as she did tennis bracelets. Jane had been the last of Sarah's affairs in a social circle of wealthy and/or celebrity lesbians. Jane's entree to the circle was money; Sarah's credential had been two Olympic competitions.

At first, Sarah had thought she'd found her niche in life, but she had tired of travel and parading to the next event where lesbians would gather. She'd also gotten tired of living on other people's money. She had her own small trust fund inherited from her mother's mother, but she couldn't spend like Jane and her friends. Center court seats at Wimbledon and passes to LPGA tournament events had gradually fallen in her list of priorities and she'd left Jane, *sans rancor*.

After years of flitting from city to city, she had longed for roots, to sink deep into one woman and one place. She gave up the glitter life without a backward glance, informed the USOC she was leaving competitive archery and buried herself in the loamy earth of Grannie MacNeil's farm in the Cascades. She had spent an entire summer and fall picking tomatoes and zucchini, canning apples, checking the hen roost for eggs and practicing with her grandmother's longbow. Her mother said she was wasting her time, but it turned out to be the last summer she and Grannie would have together, and she never regretted starting her law program at mid-year instead of the fall like her other classmates. She had long talks with Grannie about Fate and Romance and Happiness and about what Sarah should expect from life now that youth really was behind her. She had to Get Serious about Life, Grannie said. After all, she was twenty-eight and the pressures and rewards of competition were behind her.

Grannie didn't even blink when Sarah confessed her lesbianism; in fact, she told Sarah a lovely story of a lady knight who had won a widow's love and how they retired to the granite hills of Snowdon. Grannie had a real gift for story-telling and ever since Sarah could remember, she'd told romantic

14

Welsh stories in the television-free evenings with sometimes only a crackling fire to light the room.

That last summer together Sarah had felt too jaded to say she believed in Romance anymore, but she'd eaten the stories up like a starving teenager. But since Grannie died it had been harder and harder to keep hoping she'd fall in love the way Welsh Grannie had loved her American husband, the way the knight had loved her widow, the way Lady Joanna had loved Llewellyn Fawr.

When the spring semester started, she applied herself to her J.D. at the University of Washington. Grannie MacNeil died suddenly a few months later and Sarah found herself the owner of the farm and, even more precious, Grannie MacNeil's longbow. She had spent some time at the farm every year since, except for this last year, when a job promotion and a broken romance had made life too stressful for a vacation.

If she wanted to, she could blame all of the unhappiness of the past year on the promotion. She'd worked more hours, hours Ellen had come to resent, and then Sarah resented Ellen's resentment. And she resented Ellen's ex's dependence on Ellen for everything from balancing her checkbook to hurrying over in the middle of the night because Judy had heard something go bump. Ellen resented Sarah's "possessiveness" and they'd both started too many sentences with "If you really loved me, you'd . . ."

In the five years since finishing her degree and passing the bar exam, she had only been strongly attracted to Ellen, with her easy laugh and love of nature. Most of the year leading up to their break-up, Sarah worked as the lead on the patent application of a software product that was abruptly scrapped. A few weeks later, her relationship with Ellen was on the scrapheap, too. Well, the love they had both felt was long gone, if in fact it had ever existed to begin with.

Instead of Ellen, her days and weekends were filled to bursting with computer programming specifications, legal briefs and 2,500-page patent applications. It was hard for anything to survive under the weight.

Sarah realized she was standing in a daze in the middle of the hotel lobby and she shook herself mentally. A night with Jane Austen would be very refreshing and Lord knows she could use a good night's sleep. She turned resolutely to the elevators.

"Sarah, wait up."

Sarah turned and then smiled a greeting at Anna Ramos.

"I just wanted to thank you for being brave this morning," Anna said. "You have no idea how I argued —"

"I had a feeling," Sarah said. "I was happy to do it."

"Well, I know it wasn't easy, so thank you again. Are you going on the excursion?"

Sarah shook her head. "I've been to the Downs before. I thought I'd curl up with a book since I never get to do that at home."

"That sounds so tempting," Anna said. "Between the boys and that great big boy I married, not to mention the job and Association volunteer work, I haven't read a novel in years."

"With me, it's just the work in the way," Sarah said.

"To be honest, if the boys didn't clamor, I'd be a workaholic, too."

I guess I am a workaholic, Sarah told herself after she took leave of Anna. Well, she hadn't started out that way, but somewhere along the way she had

16

turned from Sarah the Archer or Sarah the Gardener into Sarah the Patent Attorney. Grannie MacNeil would not have approved.

How long had it been since she'd indulged in a hot bath, a good book and a hot fudge sundae? Work projects flowed into the bitter emptiness left by Ellen's departure and she'd pounded out a lot of her anger on her computer keyboard. Until Ellen, none of her relationships had ended in acrimony. Jane had accepted Sarah's decision to leave with a resigned smile. Jenny, the ballroom dancer, had been the one to say she thought their time was up. And before Jenny there had been lovers in college and fellow athletes — relationships that had never had any expectation of permanence. Not precisely casual, but not serious.

So why such a bitter ending with Ellen? Was it because they had both thought, for two comfortable and pleasing years and one bitter, that they were on their way to happily-ever-after?

It was a prickling along her neck that made Sarah look up from her study of the elevator floor. Someone was staring at her. It only took a moment to see who — the blond from the bar last night. She blushed as she remembered the lascivious suggestion she'd mimed and saw the blond had a slowly warming smile that became more sultry as the moments passed.

They stared at each other across the crowded elevator, remaining at opposite ends as the other passengers gradually exited. Only when they were alone did Sarah realize she'd missed her floor.

"Ohmigosh," she gasped, pressing her floor button as the elevator descended. Just in time. The doors opened and she got off, then looked over her shoulder. The blond raised her eyebrows and Sarah

17

felt another blush surge over her cheeks and she found herself smiling stupidly and feeling utterly gauche.

The blond slipped out of the elevator just as the doors closed and stood staring again, obviously enjoying Sarah's discomfiture. Sarah finally turned and began the long walk to her door. The blond fell into step behind her.

My God, Sarah thought. I'm being stalked. Her head swam a little and she realized that it had been a long time since she had felt this way in the presence of another woman. She wouldn't let herself think that this was the beginning of something meaningful, that this was the moment, the first glance that meant romance and a life of forever afters. This was not anything like that. It was lust, pure and simple, and well, why not enjoy it?

She stopped at her door and looked over her shoulder. The blond slowed her pace, but the bright gray eyes didn't falter in their persistent, increasingly intimate stare. Sarah opened the door and stepped back with an "after you" gesture. The blond passed Sarah on a waft of Pierre Cardin.

Sarah set her notebook and jacket on the chair next to the bed while the blond walked to the window and looked out at the twinkling lights of Louisville. "I think I should —"

"Don't talk if you don't want to," the blond said. "Your nonverbal communication is excellent." She turned from the window with a knowing quirk to her lips.

Beautiful lips. They made Sarah think of sunset over Puget Sound, crimson and orange and hot and cool. She shook away the fanciful image. A flesh-and-bones woman was slowly crossing the room toward her.

"Was it just bravado," the blond was murmuring. "Were you just acting curious? Or are you really wondering . . ." Warm breath tickled Sarah's ear and she caught her breath. ". . . what it would be like to be with a woman?"

Sarah opened her mouth to say she knew full well what it was like, but she said instead, "I can't go on thinking of you as 'the blond.' "

"Melissa. And you're Sarah."

"How did you — oh, the name tag."

Melissa slowly unzipped her leather jacket, revealing a close-fitting white muscle shirt that unaccountably made Sarah's mouth water. It had been too long since she'd felt the tickling fear of anticipation and the cacophony of her body waking up in all different places — tongue, ears, nipples, toes. The insides of her thighs wanted to rub together and she couldn't help but put a hand to her pitching stomach.

"I won't bite." Melissa slowly brought Sarah's hands her breasts and then sighed when Sarah cupped them. "You can't help yourself, can you?"

"No."

"I don't usually do this, but there was something about the way you danced with him and flirted with me that made me want you. And to want you to forget him."

"He's just a friend," Sarah said. Her fingertips closed on Melissa's taut nipples.

"I don't care what he is to you," Melissa said. The bright gray of her eyes had gone smoky. "I just care about right now. Oh —" Sarah's teeth found one nipple through the shirt and Melissa arched to her mouth. "You're a quick learner," she gasped.

"I've had years of planning this moment." Sarah straightened up with a private smile. It was a true statement. She only omitted that her planning had been followed by lots of practice.

"If you've been waiting for years, then I'd better make this memorable, hadn't I?" Melissa twined her hands with Sarah's, then jerked Sarah forward into her arms, her kiss hungry and demanding.

It caught Sarah off guard and she found herself arching her back so Melissa could pull her skirt up and push her pantyhose down.

Melissa groaned and broke the kiss. "This is how a man would do it, right? Take you right now. The first time would be hard and fast and then you'd do it again, slower."

"I don't know," Sarah said shakily. It didn't sound all that bad a plan, if that's what Melissa had in mind. She was shivering with desire and Melissa's hands caressing her hips and the small of her back were making her knees buckle.

"That's not how it's going to be," Melissa said. "You tell me what you want."

"I — I want you to seduce me," Sarah said, in a low voice. "I don't usually — I mean, I'm usually in charge —" She faltered, not because she was afraid Melissa would figure out she'd been with women before, but because she didn't talk about sex easily. Most of her previous lovers had expected Sarah the athlete to be the aggressor and she was used to the role. But now she wanted to be pursued, seduced, made love to.

"We're most of the way there, don't you think?" Melissa let go of Sarah and stepped back. Her hands went to her fly and she eased the buttons open and shrugged out of her jacket.

Sarah nodded mutely and bit her lower lip as Melissa stepped out of the jeans. She was long-limbed and lightly tanned. She had the firm body of someone who exercised regularly, the kind of body Sarah used to have before five years of patents had added some round curves, especially on her hips.

"Come here," Melissa said from next to the bed.

Sarah went, stepping out of her pumps and pantyhose as she took the few steps to the bed. She abandoned herself to the unreality of the moment, wondering only briefly if this was what being swept off her feet meant. She couldn't recall ever feeling this way, so eager to surrender, not even the very first time.

It seemed like hours between each button of her blouse coming undone under Melissa's fingers. In between buttons Melissa's mouth brushed over her straining breasts, her tongue flicked over the newly exposed skin, and her fingers dipped under the edge of Sarah's bra. Sarah knew she was swaying on her feet, but she could only watch each button come undone and wait, breathless, longing for the next.

Time stretched and finally Melissa pushed Sarah's blouse off her shoulders. Sarah's mouth was dry and she was lightheaded. Melissa slipped Sarah's bra straps off her shoulders and with her hands sliding under the fabric, she moved Sarah's bra down, little by little.

"Please." Sarah moaned. Her breasts were uncovered and still Melissa teased her. "I can't stand up anymore —"

Melissa's answer was to drop to her knees, her mouth so close to the place where Sarah ached that Sarah felt the gray edges of faintness. Then Melissa pulled Sarah down, sitting her on the edge of the bed. Kneeling between Sarah's legs, Melissa brought her mouth to Sarah's breasts.

"I could spend all night like this," Melissa whispered.

Sarah barely heard her. Her brain was only processing the way Melissa's tongue caressed the soft underside of her breasts, then the sharp pleasure of Melissa's teeth on her already aching nipples. A marching band could have wandered by and Sarah wouldn't have heard them. She felt as if her skin was peeling off, her nerves like wires laid bare, sparking with heat.

She didn't feel Melissa's fingers between her legs until they were already inside her. The realization made her breath catch and she felt the first tightenings of orgasm. Melissa moaned against Sarah's breasts and tightened her grip as Sarah stretched upwards, then wrapped her legs around Melissa and ground herself toward the knowing pressure of Melissa's fingers. A moment more of stillness, only her heart hammering, and she hurtled backward onto the bed, gasping for air.

After a few minutes she was able to raise her head. Melissa hadn't moved and Sarah half-expected to see a triumphant smile. But it wasn't triumph; the naked hunger on Melissa's face made Sarah feel faint again. Then she realized Melissa's fingers were still in her ... one finger moved slightly and Melissa's gaze shot upwards to Sarah's, watching the effect of that tiny movement on Sarah's face.

Sarah's lips trembled and she fell back on the bed, sinking into the delirium of Melissa's mouth on her ... at last. One finger still pressed inside her. Sarah felt like water sinking into sand and she fell deep into Melissa's hungry mouth.

Indigo became purple became crimson, then the soft light of night. Melissa had joined her on the bed, breathing softly into Sarah's ear.

Sarah got unsteadily to her feet and pulled off

what remained of her clothes. She lowered herself to Melissa's waiting body.

"You haven't left me much energy," she said softly, "but I'll do —" She nipped Melissa's thigh, then trailed her tongue over the point of Melissa's hip bone. "I'll do the best I can."

Focus — it had been a long time since she had focused so completely on a single objective. Melissa's hands were in her hair, pressing Sarah down eagerly. Sarah inhaled Melissa's scent and savored the intoxication that welled through her. She closed her eyes and let her senses guide her unerringly to the spot that made Melissa groan.

They took the bath Sarah had planned for herself, feeding each other strawberries dipped in hot fudge from the room service tray on the floor. Long, languorous kisses left no time for talking. The bath led to bed again and bed, finally, much later, to sleep.

2

Life itself is but motion, and can never be
without desire . . . (Thomas Hobbes)

Concentration for Sarah was hard in coming during the next morning's session. She would just get into the topic, *Blueprint for Patenting Ideas*, and she'd remember Melissa. She'd woken up by herself but a note on the pillow had taken away the sting. She slipped her hand into the pocket of her jacket. She didn't need to take it out to know the note still said, "See you in the elevator at lunch?"

Focus, Sarah, really. She started taking notes again and flipped to the next page in her notebook. She gasped just loud enough to attract the attention of her neighbor and hurriedly flipped the notebook closed. She knew she was blushing, but thankfully the man turned away. Branded on her mind's eye was the pencil sketch of herself, naked and asleep, with the block letters below: QUICK LEARNER.

The moment the session was out she made her way hurriedly to the elevators, glancing around for Melissa. Anna Ramos stopped her briefly to introduce her to a board member. Sarah recognized the recruiting gleam in Anna's eye, but she had no intention of joining an AAPA committee. Some people loved to do it — company travel budget and time away from the rest of the work — but Sarah really didn't much care for hotels and airplanes. Even after a few days she was hankering for the green hills of Seattle.

She had almost made it to the elevators when Geoff hallooed from across the hallway.

"Hey, good looking, have lunch with me."

"Sorry, Geoff," Sarah said, and then — dammit — she blushed. Why didn't she just take out a marker and write I GOT LUCKY LAST NIGHT on her forehead? "I have plans."

Geoff's eyebrows arched in surprise. "Do tell. You look positively guilty."

"Are you going to the procedural session this afternoon?" When Geoff nodded, she said, "I'll tell you all about it then. We can pass notes."

"Tell me more now." He began glancing around as if looking for Sarah's paramour.

"I'll be late for my appointment," Sarah said primly.

"Appointment? It's called an assignation in genteel society. Nooners in not-so-genteel circumstances. You go, girl."

Sarah gave him her very best narrow-eyed glare. I have you in my sight, she thought. Ten seconds with a longbow — hell, any kind of bow — and you'd be singing soprano, buddy.

25

"Don't give me that haughty look, I'm green with envy — ooooooh . . ." His voice trailed away as his eyes widened at the sight of something or someone behind her. "I'll let you go now. You'll just make the elevator."

"Peasant." Sarah tried and failed to hide a grin. She sprinted for the elevator and thrust her notebook between the closing doors to the annoyance of all the passengers except the grinning Melissa.

"Sorry," Sarah mumbled, and found a place on the opposite wall from Melissa.

Melissa was staring at her again, but this time Sarah returned the stare with one of her own. I have you in my sight, she thought, just as she had with Geoff. You're not going to dissolve me into a silly schoolgirl again. And you're about to find out that "quick learner" doesn't even begin to tell the story.

They were alone in the hallway as they approached Sarah's door. "Hold this for me," Sarah said, handing Melissa her notebook. It slipped through her fingers and when Melissa bent over to pick it up Sarah shamelessly ran her hands over Melissa's hips and firmly pressed her fingers into the crotch of her jeans.

Melissa gave a shocked gasp, shot to her feet and turned, completely flustered. "Rotten trick —" she began, but Sarah silenced her with a hard kiss.

She backed Melissa up to the wall and pulled her shirt out of her jeans. She got lost in the kiss and the way Melissa's ribs felt under her fingertips. She wore no bra and Sarah prickled all over.

Melissa broke the kiss with a laugh. "Don't you think it would be prudent to get out of the hallway?"

Sarah managed to back away. She'd forgotten where they were and here she'd been thinking she was totally in control of the situation. She fumbled for her room key and managed to get the door open.

Melissa held up a warning finger as she bent to pick up the notebook. "Keep your distance," she warned.

Once inside they looked at each other, Sarah feeling suddenly very shy. Melissa was looking at her feet. Sarah said softly, "I'm feeling a fraud, you know."

"Because when you go back home you'll be going back to your boyfriend or husband or whatever?"

"No," Sarah said, sheepishly. "Because I'm too chicken to say what I feel. And because I sort of misled you — I always have been and always will be a lesbian." Melissa's mouth opened to a tiny O. "Though it's hard to believe, some lesbians grow up to be patent attorneys."

"Well, that explains a few things. You — well. You really —" Melissa's blush was adorable. "I mean, last night, you were amazing."

"I don't do this, you know. I don't even know your last name."

"Hartley," Melissa said, her blush fading. She looked intently at Sarah and said, "You were saying something about being chicken."

Sarah nodded. "I feel like we should have lunch, talk about our lives and all that. So this will be a little more civilized."

"I don't feel very civilized," Melissa said.

"Neither do I." Sarah moved a few steps closer to her. "I'm just not the kind of person to say, 'Baby, let's go to bed' to someone I just met."

"But that's exactly what you want to do, isn't it?"

"Oh, yes." She gave Melissa a cheeky smile. "That's precisely what I want to do."

"Well then let's pretend we've had some civilized conversations and we both respect each other as individuals and that we're not really here for one thing and one thing only." Melissa closed the distance between them, standing close enough for Sarah to smell her tantalizing cologne.

"I think I can do that," Sarah said weakly. She mirrored Melissa's movements by removing her jacket and shoes, then her hose when Melissa stepped out of her jeans, and her blouse when Melissa pulled her polo shirt over her head. A few steps took her to Melissa's arms and they fell together on the bed.

Melissa's mouth was on her breasts, savoring them with the slow attention that Sarah was fast realizing she had always craved. "I'm so glad you've never been with men," Melissa said. "We weren't exactly safe last night."

"That's no guarantee I'm safe," Sarah said.

Over her languid sigh, Melissa said, "I have the feeling you're anything but safe for me."

Sarah wanted to laugh but Melissa's tongue snaked its way across her stomach. "Even if I were straight I think I'd be changing my mind right about now."

It wasn't like last night, it couldn't be. Not a tidal wave, but a gentle, persistent crest, at times fierce, and oh so delectable. She savored Melissa's mouth on her, then took her own time returning the pleasure.

Sarah had no idea what time it was when they finally curled side by side on the bed. So she'd missed the afternoon session. Half the attorneys at the conference were out golfing. This was more fun. She gently pulled on Melissa's earlobe, liking the tiny silver labrys that pierced it. She hadn't seen one in years. "Where do you live?"

Melissa stretched thoroughly, like a cat, and said, "I'm cabin-sitting for some friends and you've never heard of the closest town."

"Try me," Sarah said. Her mind readied itself to calculate air fares.

"Suquamish."

Deep, deep down inside, Sarah felt what was left of her belief in Romance and Happiness start a conga line. "So it's what, forty minutes to the Bremerton ferry?"

Melissa raised up on one elbow. "Where do you live?"

"Snoqualmie. On a good day that's only thirty minutes from the ferry landing in Seattle."

"Let's skip the afternoon sessions and have some lunch," Melissa said. "I am really hungry."

"I thought we were pretending not to be civilized." Sarah watched as Melissa reclaimed her clothes.

"We've got all the time in the world to be civilized now. That is, if you'd like to see me back home."

"Even if I had to swim Puget Sound myself."

Melissa stood smiling at her, the gray in her eyes gleaming silver. Even though Sarah sternly told them not to, Romance and Happiness continued their conga line, adding Fate to the celebrants.

Debra said, "Where are you off to in such a hurry? Big weekend plans?"

"I'm picking someone up at the ferry and I don't want to be late." The last thing Sarah needed was an interrogation from Debra.

"Anyone I know? Of course not, I don't know

anybody. So — does this person have anything to do with the little hop in your step for the last week and a half?"

"I don't know what you mean."

Debra crossed her brown eyes and said, "Give me a break. You think I'm dumb or something?"

Sarah's lips twitched as she picked up her briefcase. It was full of work, but she doubted she'd have a moment to do any of it. She planned to spend every moment with Melissa. She shooed Debra back out of her office and headed for the elevator. Debra followed, her heels clicking on the lobby tiles. Sarah only looked at her after she pushed the call button. Every inch of Debra quivered like a curious poodle.

"You've got to tell me something, or I'll just die before Monday! A name, anything."

"Melissa," Sarah said patiently.

"Melissa Etheridge?" Debra's eyes were like dinner plates. "That's why you're being so secretive! She and Julie are mommies! This is really, really bad karma."

Sarah rolled her eyes. "Keeping jumping to conclusions like that and you'll sprain something."

"What am I supposed to think when you won't tell me anything? I don't have a life, I have to live through yours. And lately yours has been as dull as mine. I'm going to go nuts."

With anyone else Sarah would have been irritated. With Debra she wrinkled her nose and said, "Good. You're a little too sane to work here. I'm not saying another word."

As the elevator doors closed Debra said, "You'll pay for this, Sarah MacNeil. I better get a full report on Monday or else I'll —"

As the elevator descended Sarah mentally finished the sentence. Or she'll make my life a living hell.

* * * * *

Willowy. That was the word Sarah had been searching for ever since Geoff called Melissa "cute." She'd never really understood what willowy meant until Melissa walked across the pier toward her, blond locks lifting in the sea wind, pencil-leg jeans clinging to every curve of her calves and thighs, and the ever-present bomber jacket unzipped to the waist. Even the knapsack didn't ruin the elegant sway of her hips. No, not beautiful, not really even cute, but incredibly attractive to Sarah's eyes.

Melissa swept her into a warm embrace, then after a small hesitation, she kissed Sarah full on the mouth. The kiss lengthened until Sarah self-consciously broke away. The ferry pier in Seattle was not the best place for two women to make out. She took Melissa's suitcase and noticed they had attracted some leering attention, but in truth most of the passengers and dock workers were going about their business. Still, once they were in the car, Sarah lost no time putting some distance between them and the pier.

"Nice car," Melissa said. She ran one finger over the teak dash.

"I bought this car the day after I paid off my last student loan. I didn't want a sedan, at least not yet. I guess I thought I wasn't old enough." The Jaguar XJS was conservative on the outside until the top went down. On the stretch of I-90 between Seattle and Spokane, which took her out to Grannie MacNeil's farm, she sometimes opened it up to as much as 160 when the highway was deserted. Claire, after Jenny, before Jane, had raced as a part of the Jaguar team.

31

"It's you," Melissa said. "Deceptive on the outside."

"Why thanks," Sarah said, taking the shortest route to I-90 to cross Mercer Island. It was a warm, late summer afternoon with leaves in deepening green blowing in the sea wind that had cleared yesterday's clouds. "I thought you were going to compare me to the motor or something. You know, runs hot, fast idle, lots of get up and go."

"Well, it's all true, just not my style of compliments." Melissa turned away from the panorama of Lake Union nestled against evergreen hills. "God, it's good to see you."

"I feel exactly the same way," Sarah said. "I was half afraid you would change your mind and —"

"Weren't sure your heart would go pitty pat when you saw me?"

"I was never in doubt about my feelings," Sarah said, shooting a happy grin across the car.

"So why would you doubt mine?" Melissa slid one hand slowly over Sarah's denim-covered knee. Then it slid upwards and Sarah involuntarily opened her thighs. She sighed with a smile, then her foot slipped off the gas pedal.

"Enough of that," Sarah said. "Let's get home in one piece."

"Whatever you say," Melissa said. "I really deserve a break because I worked very hard this week."

"Doing what?"

"More than twenty women asked for a precis of my documentary project at the writer's conference, so I wrote it and sent them out. I'm hoping I'll get a grant to do it. Marsha Davis, the executive director of the Rainbow Foundation, was particularly interested."

"That sounds exciting," Sarah said. "What's your documentary about?"

"It's a survey of lesbian-created art, particularly video and film. Photography, too. I want to focus on lesbian works with no male influences."

"If they're lesbian-created where does the male influence come in? I mean of course virtually everything a lesbian may do is influenced by male society — from Michelangelo to art history classes, and so on."

"I'm more interested in the act of creation than the outcome. If a lesbian focused her energies and life to be separate from men and ended up painting just like Michelangelo I would still be interested, because her process and her struggle to have a lesbian identity would be the real story."

"Oh." Sarah didn't quite get it. "But if the work is just like Michelangelo's how does it become Lesbian art with a big L?"

"That's just what I mean." Melissa bounced enthusiastically in her seat. "It's not Lesbian art, whatever that is, but Lesbian-Created art." She threw a grin at Sarah. "Big L, Big C. I've got lots of ideas but never had any money to put them out there."

"That's a common complaint. Orson Welles had to beg, borrow and steal to produce *Citizen Kane* because he wanted to do it outside the studio system." Sarah found making conversation a little difficult, not because she wasn't interested in what Melissa was working on, but because Melissa's hand still rested lightly on her thigh.

"Well, I'm *really* outside the studio system. Not

33

that I'd want to be inside. As soon as you walk in the door there are men everywhere who can't wait to take your ideas and tone them down for mass market, and the women are almost as bad. There have been so many writers I admired and when they went mainstream they weren't worth reading any more. I want to make it big, but I still want to be a real lesbian when I'm done."

Sarah swerved out from behind a van that had decided to move into the fast lane and slow down. "Just what is a real lesbian?" It had been a long time since she'd thought about the politics of being a lesbian.

"Well, a real lesbian doesn't have anything to do with men."

"What about a woman who realizes she's a lesbian after she's been with men?"

"Well, she's a lesbian, but not . . . well, maybe *real* isn't the right word. It just seems like those of us who always knew have a different outlook."

"You're probably right," Sarah said. "I always knew, but one outlook isn't necessarily more valid than another. It's just that we've all walked a different path to the same place."

"I'm not sure we're in the same place. Case in point — I was working on an anthology with a woman I thought was a real lesbian. We needed some money to keep going and she went to her ex-husband — I didn't even know she'd been married. I thought we had a lot in common. When I found out, I bailed and the real bitch of it is that she got it published and all the credit and all the money, when a lot of the work was mine. I don't want to get burned again by a woman whose first instinct is to run to a man for help."

"How did where the money came from change the content of your book?"

"You sound just like she did." Melissa looked out her window with a small frown.

"I don't mean to," Sarah said, alarmed. "I do spend a lot of every day with men, but I don't think I'm less of a lesbian for it."

Melissa's frown lifted. "I have to admit that your credentials are not in question." She traced a line along Sarah's thigh with a lazy finger.

"I'm glad you had a productive week," Sarah said, trying to change the subject. "I had to really buckle down, but I managed to get through some work."

"I also took some photos of some of the big names at the conference and sent a proof sheet to *Curve* and *The Advocate*. Maybe they'll buy a photo or two. The cash would be good. I had to do it anyway since I got into the conference on a press pass. Then I was so jazzed I think I sent out almost a hundred precis of my novel. My second one, not the first. I think I'm going to have to rewrite the first one because I can't seem to find a market for it. But I don't want to change it just to sell it. This guy I met at Putnam said it had too many women in it and since there were some straight women, why weren't there any men? Talk about clueless."

Sarah didn't ask what she really wanted to know, which was if Melissa had published anything. She didn't want to sound like she thought publishing was the only proof of worth when she knew perfectly well that a lot of fine writers languished undiscovered for years. Instead, she asked, "Have you been trying to publish it for a long time?"

"Ages. About three years. I wrote it in college, when I was coming out and discovered the underground society of women. Have you ever noticed that women know where to gather? And they naturally gather together? Not all women, but those who are less involved with clubs or men. For instance, the liberal arts majors and non-sorority women."

"I know what you mean. The women athletes always have a place where they go —"

"And it's not quite the same place as I mean," Melissa said. "The jocks —"

"Are you calling me a jock?" Sarah arched her eyebrows in mock anger and accelerated hard when the van finally merged back out of the lane.

Melissa flushed. "I don't mean it as an insult."

"I'm teasing," Sarah said. "I was a jock. And I noticed that while we jocks were sitting in the student union drinking our beer, there were a lot of really interesting-looking women hanging out near the salad bar. I always assumed they were what was left of the Women's Center."

"They probably were," Melissa said. "The centers may have closed over the years, but the need is still there. For a separate space that's not about men and dating and —"

"Oh, now I always assumed that there was a lot of angst about dating, just not about dating men."

Melissa laughed. "You've got me there. But it's a different kind of angst. Not as angry, not as desperate."

Sarah didn't say that she'd seen some desperate lesbian relationships. The woman in Jane's life right before Sarah had been desperate when the relationship ended with Sarah's entrance, desperate to find someone, anyone who would keep her in the merry-go-round of Jane's social circle — where everyone was a celebrity of some sort or another and non-celebrity girlfriends were left behind after the relationship had run its course. In the end, Sarah hadn't liked the casualness of it — the way affairs always ended with a wave of a hand and both partners wondering what kind of woman they'd hook up with next. Seeded tennis players and pro golfers were always in great demand.

Melissa was saying, "So I concentrated on making it a snapshot in time. The way a lot of women living in the outer streams were shaping their lives and society. That's what it's called — Outerstream. As opposed to mainstream."

"What's your second novel about?"

"Living on borrowed time. Which is what I feel like most of the time."

"Why?" Sarah stole a glance at Melissa, who was shrugging her shoulders.

"I want to write and photograph and document our lives. But those aren't things you can make a ready living at, not when the topic is lesbians. So I housesit and find space in collectives and keep moving. I'm afraid I'll get stale if I stay in one place for a long time, but I'm always worried about where I'll go next. I could have stayed a year at a ranch in South Dakota, but there was no electricity — you know, real separatists, living like the Amish — and my computer, ancient though it is, needs electricity. There was an editor at Simon and Schuster who was interested in a story about separatists, too. I can't imagine trying to write in longhand though I know until the last hundred years that's exactly how everyone wrote."

"No electricity is a little too rustic for me, too."

"And then there's the bathing thing. Heating my own hot water was not my idea of a luxurious bath."

Sarah laughed. "My grandmother lived pretty much that way till the day she died. She had electricity the last twenty years of her life, but other than that she had a very simple, natural way. But she always maintained that everyone deserved hot running water. She remembered the date and time it was installed in her cabin and celebrated it the way some people celebrate the Fourth of July. She was quite a character."

"I think people should live more simply than they do," Melissa said seriously, "or rather that we could all live more simply than we do. I like living in the cabin, though it's lonely sometimes. I drive over to the market for what I need and the woodpile is still plenty tall. The people who lent me the cabin are housesitting for friends in New York who are housesitting for friends in Venice — and so on. I've got it definitely through the winter, maybe until June."

"It sounds lovely." Sarah accelerated to avoid traffic merging in from the 405, then settled into the number one lane on the Sunset Highway, skirting Lake Sammamish to the south. "We'll be at my place in fifteen minutes or so."

"This area is gorgeous," Melissa said. "The cabin is spectacular, too. You'll definitely have to come visit."

Sarah sternly told Fate to be quiet and to please stop Romance from singing all the verses of "I Think I Love You." Nauseating song.

They chatted about the passing scenery and their mutual love of Washington State. In no time at all, Sarah pulled into her driveway and opened the garage door with the remote. She suddenly felt nervous about showing Melissa the house. She was definitely a decadent capitalist, but she did try to do her part in the world — she supported planting trees and ending clear-cutting, preserving the old growth forests that were left, and she'd lent money to the Seattle Community Loan Fund. The house she'd bought, however, didn't really reflect her greener instincts. She'd bought it solely for the view of Mt. Snoqualmie from the living room and a backyard that was narrow but long.

"What a beautiful house," Melissa said. "Wow." She stopped at the entrance to the living room. At the far end the 6,300-foot mountain was framed in an uncurtained window. The near western face was granite interspersed with evergreens; snow still clung to the northern face. The upper twenty percent of the mountain was ringed with haze and fog, defying the otherwise brilliant blue skies.

It was mystical and pure, Sarah thought, and the long, populated valley between her and the mountain mattered not at all.

"How romantic," Melissa said. "It's very inspiring."

"I think so," Sarah said. When she first moved in she'd spent hours shooting in the backyard. The mountain in the backdrop had always put her in the mood of Robin Hood or her Grannie's legends of Welsh archers who had turned away Norman invaders from the foot of Eyri. She realized she hadn't been in the backyard since early spring, when she'd dug a surprise snowfall out from around the less hardy plants. A gardening service kept the yard in good condition and she'd been snowed under at work. Her shoulder muscles twinged and she knew she'd pay for it the next time she drew a bow.

"What are you thinking," Melissa asked. "I can't read you sometimes."

Sarah picked up Melissa's suitcase and said, "I'm thinking it's time to show you the bedroom."

Showing Melissa the bedroom took several hours

— delightful and passionate hours that wiped away the last of Sarah's anxiety that what she and Melissa had discovered in Louisville couldn't happen at home. It happened.

"Wonderful," is what Sarah whispered to Melissa as they lay side by side.

"Oh yeah," Melissa said emphatically. "Wonderful hardly seems adequate."

"How about some dinner? I laid in a supply of Chinese food so we wouldn't have to go out tonight. I'm not much of a cook. I mean, I can cook, but I don't have the time to do it properly. I know how to can apples in a thunderstorm but it takes preparation."

"A useful skill," Melissa said, tracing Sarah's shoulder with one lazy finger. "Being a vegetarian, I do cook for myself a lot. Living in a remote place makes me grateful for anyone else's cooking, and restaurants. But at least living right on the Sound I get seafood that is absolutely fresh."

"Well, tonight I have mu shu vegetables, pineapple shrimp and hot and sour soup — without meat."

"Sounds delicious and I'm starved," Melissa said.

After dinner Sarah again felt awkward. In Louisville they'd never wondered what to do with their evenings. They had made love until they were worn out, slept, ate, went to workshops late and left them early, then made love again. Now that they didn't have to make the most of every moment, suggesting they go back to bed seemed crass, though several influential parts of her body didn't agree with that assessment. "Would you like to watch a movie? I've got quite a collection."

"Sounds great," Melissa said. She turned suddenly. "You're nervous. Don't be. You don't have to play hostess."

"I can't help it." How could she say that she was afraid something would go wrong? That she was afraid they would end up indifferent to each other or discover an irreconcilable difference? She didn't want to deal with all the implications of her fears — they told her she was more attracted to Melissa than ever.

"Well, I'll have to put you at your ease, somehow," Melissa said, taking Sarah's hand. She trailed the tip of her tongue over Sarah's wrist.

"That hardly helps my composure," Sarah said, aware that the robe she had slipped on was slipping off again.

Melissa let her go and wrapped Sarah's robe tightly around her. "Let's watch a movie."

I feel like a kid, Sarah thought. She watched Melissa looking through the video collection and wondered how she, so in control of her life, with a good head on her shoulders (Grannie MacNeil's highest praise), could be reduced to pudding by a woman at least six years her junior who had lived in a somewhat sheltered, academic world. Someone who looked at Sarah as if she knew her, right down to the best and worst.

"What are you doing with all these *Die Hard* movies?" Melissa's nose was wrinkled in distaste.

"I like them," Sarah admitted sheepishly. "I know they're macho and violent. I edited out the worst of the blood and guts, but I like the writing and the production."

"But Bruce Willis is a Republican."

"Well, that was enough to turn me off Schwarzenegger movies, except for the *Terminator* ones. Him I can't stand. And the writing isn't very good. Whereas the *Die Hard* movies, well, I like them. What can I say?"

Melissa pursed her lips and gave Sarah a smile

that meant she believed she could change Sarah's mind about them. But she merely held out a cassette for inspection. "I hate to admit this, but I've never seen it."

Sarah grinned, glad that Melissa had missed her pointless yet complete collection of bad science fiction films á là Mystery Science Theater. "I'd love to see it again."

They settled down with Melissa's head on Sarah's lap to watch *Desert Hearts*.

"I finally understand," Melissa said, when Kay miscounted her change while Patsy Cline crooned "Sweet Dreams."

"Understand what?"

"Why women love this movie." She smiled up at Sarah. "The writing's good and the production is terrific."

"The novel was different, but still, the movie does it justice. There *were* men involved, I do believe."

Melissa stuck out her tongue at Sarah. "But we'll never know what it could have been if they hadn't been involved."

"I like it just the way it is," Sarah said.

Melissa was silent until the middle of what was, in Sarah's opinion, the hottest sex scene ever filmed between women. "They can't possibly be having orgasms," Melissa said.

"Who cares," Sarah breathed. She ignored Melissa's knowing smile, but she didn't object when Melissa wangled a hand under her robe.

"You have a point," Melissa said. She nibbled at Sarah's thigh through her robe.

What with the distractions that followed they had to watch the end of the movie again the next morning.

* * * * *

"Look at the roses in those cheeks!" Debra stood accusingly in Sarah's office doorway. "Now spill your guts, or else."

"What do you want to know?" Sarah exuded the patient manner she knew would madden Debra even more.

"Everything, you nit." She sat down in the guest chair with the air of someone who wasn't moving for as long as it took. "Where did you meet?"

"At the conference."

"Another patent attorney?" Debra's eyes were round.

"No. She was at a different conference."

"You're being a pain. Are we friends? Do I have to cross-examine you?"

Sarah sighed in as long-suffering a manner as she could, but she knew the tiny quirk to her lips betrayed her. "Okay. She was at a lesbian writer's conference."

"Oh, my God. Talk about luck."

"We hit it off from the start, especially after she found out I wasn't straight."

"Was this before or after you ... umm ... hit it off?"

"After. It was a little misunderstanding. She forgave me."

"I know I'm missing the whole story," Debra said. "But anyway, so where does she live? Is she famous?" Debra gasped. "It's that writer who lives on Vashon Island, the famous one, that's why you didn't want to say who and had to meet the ferry. But I thought she had a girlfriend she'd been with for years. You're a homewrecker!"

"Debra, I am not a homewrecker. Her name is Melissa Hartley and she's not famous yet and I think I'm in way over my head, okay? Is that enough detail?"

Debra looked a little disappointed. "Over your head? What do you mean?"

"It took me eighteen months to even feel like I could live with Ellen, and I loved her a lot. A part of me still does. But I wanted to ask Melissa this weekend. I haven't even known her for a month. I've been thinking about it all morning."

"Wow. You are completely bonker kitties over her."

Sarah laughed. "What the hell are bonker kitties?"

"Don't change the subject. Why can't I meet someone and fall in love?"

"I think that's the easy part," Sarah said. "It's what comes next that's the hardest."

Debra looked confused.

"Happily ever after. Monogamy."

"Nobody has happily ever after anymore. Except maybe Joanne Woodward and Paul Newman. Besides, monogamy is patriarchal."

"A wise lesbian, I don't remember which one, once said that it was the have-nots who are always in favor of redistribution."

"Oh, I see. If I ever had a serious relationship I'd turn monogamous? Thanks very much." Debra sniffed. "You think I have no courage of my convictions."

"I didn't mean it that way," Sarah began, but Debra stood up with a flounce.

"See if I care if she breaks your heart. You want something that's just not going to happen and make fun of me because I accept the world as it is." With a loud "hmph" she departed in high dudgeon.

"Shit," Sarah said. Working with Debra was like having a thoroughbred poodle around. One misstep and it would take two lunches and a box of See's Candy to repair the damage.

She tried to concentrate on her work, but reading the detailed specs for their latest operating system product was giving her a headache. Usually she could plow right into it and lift her head six hours later. Where was her focus?

In a little cabin right on Puget Sound, she thought. After she'd gotten over her jitters, she and Melissa had settled in for a lovely weekend. She rented them bicycles in Elizabeth Park and then they wended their way through Pike's Market. They found a lovely lesbian-run bistro near the university for dinner, then slept late on Sunday. They read the paper, devoured smoked salmon with bagels and cream cheese, then walked down the hill to the market for fresh salads to take on a picnic. After the picnic, Melissa admitted that it would really help if she could wash her clothes from the weekend since laundry facilities were rather primitive at her cabin. Having no clothes to wear, not even undies, Melissa complained of vulnerability, so Sarah had joined her in nakedness and before she knew it they were making love on the living room floor, as eager and as breathless as the first time.

Staring at her work wasn't accomplishing anything. She went out for lunch, something she rarely did, and tried to put Melissa out of her mind. She was still behind from having been at the conference and would only be able to take Friday off if she managed to get through some work. Granted, she had no one looking over her shoulder, but she knew what her deadlines were and knew herself well enough to know what she had to do when in order to meet them. Her boss wouldn't care if she took a month off as long as her deadlines for completing the patent applications were met. It was a plain and simple management relationship and she liked it. If she wanted to play this weekend with an extra day at the cabin with Melissa, she had to concentrate.

It was hard to concentrate when she got back to work, but she managed. She read for several hours, taking notes on her laptop of specific language she wanted to cite from the detailed specs. She finally got up for a cup of the vile coffee from the office machine, then moseyed around to Debra's office to leave the Snickers bar she'd bought at lunch. As usual, Debra was on the speakerphone — every litigation attorney Sarah knew had been born with a speakerphone — and mouthed, "You're still in trouble," as Sarah slipped the bar onto the corner of Debra's desk.

Back in her chair, she settled down for the long haul and managed to finish one set of specs before her tiny anniversary clock chimed nine o'clock. She locked up her notebook and laptop in the fireproof cabinet designed for them and drove home feeling relieved not to have lost the day in dreams about Melissa.

She didn't really think about Melissa until after she'd ordered her favorite fast food late-night snack. A burger and the salad leftovers at home would be perfect. She was waiting for her burger at the drive-thru when she remembered Melissa asking her what she had meant, their first time together, when she had said she was usually "in charge" in bed.

The memory made her weak all over. She'd straddled Melissa's waist and pinned her wrists to the floor with her hands. She kissed Melissa slowly and deeply, then said in her ear, "Because I was an athlete the non-athletic women expected me to be like this. On top. I didn't mind." She bit Melissa's earlobe, then trailed the tip of her tongue down Melissa's collarbone.

"I can't say I mind, either," Melissa said. "I just didn't see you as butch."

Sarah stopped what she was doing and looked down into Melissa's eyes. "I've never seen myself as butch either. I'm not sure I equate sexual aggressiveness with being butch. Or femme. But it's what some of my lovers expected."

"I've never been enamored of either role myself," Melissa said. "But what about —" She slipped her wrists out of Sarah's grasp and Sarah found herself on her back, with Melissa straddling her. "Top and bottom?"

Sarah started to smile, then caught her breath as Melissa's tongue grazed one nipple. "I'm okay there until pain is involved. I'm not into pain. That's why I was a lousy long distance runner."

"So far we're batting a thousand," Melissa said. "I like this — being in control for a while, doing what I want and guessing what you want. And I do like it when you're in control. When you're aggressive."

"Well," Sarah had managed, fighting the breathlessness she was beginning to associate with her want of Melissa, "now that we've decided we're sexually compatible, could we get on with it?"

"Certainly," Melissa had said, leaning down to kiss Sarah. She didn't release Sarah's wrists until she needed her hands to tease Sarah's breasts. She had stretched out next to Sarah so Sarah could turn her head and take one breast into her mouth.

Something white banged into the car window and Sarah yelped in fright. Her foot slipped off the brake and the car shot forward a few feet.

47

"Lady, your burger," the clerk snapped when Sarah rolled down her window.

"Sorry," she mumbled, and she backed up to take the bag.

No matter how you slice it, she thought as she drove away, she had it bad for Melissa. It could even be terminal.

3

A time to embrace ... (Ecclesiastes 3:6)

The ferry ride from Seattle to Bremerton took only 35 minutes and saved her over two hours of driving. Sarah spent the sailing in the bow of the ferry, letting the sea air whip through her hair and blow away all the cobwebs of the work week. She had spent every day with her nose in the specs and every night wondering what Melissa was doing, if Melissa was thinking about her as well. Last night she'd stayed at work until midnight, then left with "Walking on Sunshine" playing in her head.

The late-summer air was moist from this morning's rain and her cheeks stung from the sea wind. She watched the approaching shoreline, feeling as if she were watching her future approach, little by little, but was still too far away to make out anything specific.

She'd broken down last night and called Melissa, ostensibly to ask if she should bring her car. Melissa admitted her own transportation was not nearly as reliable as Sarah's, so the Jaguar was down in the ferry's belly. They had chatted in fits and starts and all of Sarah's fears returned when making conversation turned difficult. But Melissa said into one silence, "I'm not that great on the phone. I keep thinking about what I'd rather be doing, that is, if you were here."

"Me, too," Sarah said. "I mean thinking about what I'd rather be doing. I've been thinking about it a lot."

Melissa laughed easily and then they had hung up. Sarah felt much better but was still a little nervous.

Focus, she told herself. She couldn't hit the broadside of a barn in this mental state. Focus. Sight. Fly. She repeated the mantra of her archery, but it didn't help as much as it should have. Focus — she thought of Melissa. Focused on the sensation of her hands filled with Melissa's hair. Sight — not a bulls-eye, but Melissa's eyes, inviting, sensuous. Fly — she wanted to be the arrow, soaring across the space between them to bury herself in Melissa's warmth and lovemaking.

Nothing had ever interfered with her ability to concentrate before. Nothing and no one. Her mother had made an embarrassing scene in front of Sarah's teammates just before her first Olympic trials, but once Sarah strung her bow she hadn't thought of her mother until it was all over and she'd made her first Olympic team. Then she had an all-out fight with her that fifteen years later still wasn't repaired. To this day her mother insisted that archery had been a colossal waste of time.

So why did Melissa intrude? God knew the sex was fantastic, the best of her life. But she'd never thought of herself as a wholly sexual being and couldn't believe she'd waited 35 years to find it out. There must be another explanation for her obsession with Melissa, she thought, and the most logical explanation was a four-letter word.

She returned to her car when the ferry docked and drove into the Bremerton outskirts, then turned north on 16, which zipped right along until just outside Poulsbo. Then she drove along a narrow highway through the mixed fir and aspen, following the signs to Suquamish. With Melissa's directions it only took a few more minutes before she was turning into a graveled drive and feeling overwhelmed at the sight of Melissa running from the front door to the car, opening Sarah's door before she'd even fully stopped.

Their embrace was so exuberant that Sarah lost her footing and they both fell laughing onto the soft carpet of pine needles, then lay there panting and still laughing. Sarah thought, it's been a long time since I've felt this alive.

The cabin turned out to be less rustic than Sarah expected. It was a luxury cottage compared to Grannie MacNeil's little home. There was a large central room and a Jacuzzi just outside the back door, a modern kitchen and a large master bedroom flanked by two more bedrooms. The washing machine worked, Melissa explained, but the dryer had mysteriously decided to spin only cold air. With the weather turning cold it meant drying clothes next to the wood stove, and she'd already scorched two shirts and her favorite socks.

Sarah assured Melissa she would not need to do laundry. They snacked on the contents of the picnic basket Sarah had brought with her, then went for a walk along the highway, turning east on a little path that ran down to the shore.

The sun had already dropped below the mountains behind them, and the last of its rays were glinting off the buildings of downtown Seattle, just across the Sound to the south. The lights were coming up and they sat until the city glowed. From the water came wind laden with the scent of salt and kelp and fish. The pine trees moved against the sky with a dull roar that took Sarah back to her earliest memories of Grannie MacNeil's farm.

Sarah breathed in the aroma of the sea. "I can see why you love this place."

"It's very inspiring. I'm thinking of writing an essay about solitude and creativity. I bounced the idea off one of the judges of the Lammy Awards and she thought it could be interesting."

"Lammy Awards?"

"The Lambda Book Awards for gay and lesbian writers, publishers and editors. Being a judge is very prestigious."

Sarah digested that information, reflecting that there were parts of the community she knew nothing about. Too many patents. "Am I interfering with your writing by staying the weekend?"

"Of course not," Melissa said, leaning over to kiss her. "You are also inspiring. Inspiration is important to me.",

Sarah was a little ashamed of her blatant fishing for a compliment. "Shucks. That's just what I wanted to hear."

"Besides, I haven't been writing much. My computer is kind of quirky and it sometimes works better if I leave it alone for a while."

"That doesn't sound good," Sarah said. "It only boots when the moon is full?"

"Something like that," Melissa said with a laugh. "I don't know if there's anything you can do for it. I mean, you use a computer at work, don't you?"

"All day, but I'm not really a systems wizard. But I can take a look."

Their walk back to the cabin was companionably silent. They held hands as they crossed the highway and only broke their grasp when Melissa picked up her mail from the old-fashioned rural mailbox at the foot of the gravel drive.

Sarah loved the sound of their footsteps crunching. She and Melissa were alone in a world of green and wood, and she felt more at peace than she had in months.

Sarah found the bed in the master bedroom comfortable, especially after a long soak in the Jacuzzi and mutually satisfactory massage and lovemaking. She was awakened by a creak of the bedroom floor and opened her eyes as the scent of coffee tickled her nose.

"That's a wunnerful sight," Sarah said. "A woman with a cup of coffee in her hand."

"A cup of coffee meant for you, no less." Melissa put the mug down on the bedside table. "I'm out of milk, but I did remember sugar."

"That's okay," Sarah said. "It'll get my heart started." Actually, Melissa in a skimpy bathrobe had gotten her heart started.

Melissa said something about toast and padded back out to the kitchen. Sarah fumbled in her suitcase for the set of sweats she'd brought with her and pulled on a pair of thick socks. Melissa didn't seem to feel the cold.

When she got to the kitchen she found out why — the wood stove heated the entire kitchen and living room to a pleasant temperature.

"Toast," Melissa said, indicating the short stack on the table. "The marmalade is made locally."

"You forgot about your mail," Sarah said, sweeping the small pile off the sofa where Melissa had tossed it the night before. She deposited the mail in front of Melissa and helped herself to toast which she liberally smeared with the marmalade.

"Thanks," Melissa said. "Bill. Bill. Ooh, letter from a publisher."

"Good news, I hope," Sarah said after Melissa had studied the letter for a minute.

"Maybe. I met this woman from McGraw-Hill by chance at a conference on lesbians and the pro-choice movement. She's a big donor to Planned Parenthood. She says that she sent my query on to an editor who might consider a genre fiction project. Hmmm. I wish she'd given me that person's name."

"Well, she forwarded it, which is helpful." Sarah licked her thumb free of the gooey apple-orange marmalade. A large swallow of coffee made her feel almost human.

"That's true," Melissa said brightly. "She really seemed to appreciate my work. We hit it off from the start. Oh, a letter from my friends, the ones I'm housesitting for. They've been sending me postcards and little updates about the fun they're having in New York. The place they're staying is right in the Village."

"New York is a nice place to visit, but —" Sarah broke off when Melissa made a noise of surprise and alarm.

"They're coming back," she said. "Their friends in Venice decided to come home early and my friends want to spend the rest of their sabbatical here. They say I'm welcome to stay, but ... it won't be the same." She stared at the letter and Sarah realized tears were swimming in the corners of Melissa's eyes.

Everything went into slow motion for Sarah. Her own breathing sounded loud in her ears. Her vision narrowed and she saw only Melissa. Nothing else in the world existed — she had found her moment of focus. Melissa was in her sight. She had only to let fly and trust the path of the arrow.

"Come live with me," she said. "I've got lots of room."

Melissa looked up at her in surprise. "You hardly know me —"

"I know you very well, in the Biblical sense," Sarah said, trying to smile. Her heart was hammering painfully against her sternum.

"That's not the same," Melissa said. "I — I don't know what to say."

"Say yes."

"I — you're being very generous."

"Say yes," Sarah said again.

"Are you asking because you have lots of room, or —"

"I'm asking because I want to be near you more than just weekends. I would like to wake up with you every day." Sarah's throat tightened and she managed to choke out, "Please say yes."

"Yes," Melissa said.

"Are you out of your mind?" Debra almost levitated out of her chair. "She's moving in with you?"

"I know," Sarah said. "I think if I listened closely, I'd hear some part of myself screaming in fear. But I can't stop smiling. Every time I think of her I smile and get these fluttery butterflies." Common Sense told Sarah she was babbling. Romance told Common Sense to shut up.

"You're acting like an adolescent."

"No, I've fallen in love."

"It's practically the same thing," Debra said, crushingly. "Love. What is it? Ladies and gentlemen of the jury, I submit to you that love is a construct invented to explain otherwise mad behavior to your friends. I can't believe you asked her to live with you just because she was getting the boot from her housesit. I can see why she said yes —"

"I know exactly why she said yes." Sarah was starting to be annoyed.

"Did you actually see the postmark? Maybe she wrote the letter to herself. Free rent —"

"Debra, don't do this!" Sarah felt an unfamiliar flash of anger.

"Do what? I'm just trying to be sensible, but you won't let me get a word in edgewise."

"Don't make me choose between you and her. Because I'll choose her."

"Geez-us-Christ." Debra fumed across Sarah's desk. "I can't wait to meet her."

"Not with that attitude, you won't."

"Attitude? Attitude? Who's got the attitude here?" Debra spoke through clenched teeth. "You go off to some conference, have a grand boff with some bimbo, and now you've given her the keys to your house?" Debra got to her feet. "But hey, it's your decision. I respect that."

"Thank you," Sarah said sarcastically.

"I can't wait to meet your lady love. I'll be on best behavior."

"I'm glad to hear it. Come to dinner next Wednesday. She'll be all settled by then." Sarah couldn't help her waspish tone.

"Thank you, I'd be delighted," Debra replied just as waspishly. She flounced out of Sarah's office. But this time, Sarah thought, she owes *me* the chocolate.

"I thought you could use this room as your office and storage. I cleaned out most of my junk. Those are the boxes I brought back with me." Sarah studied Melissa's expression anxiously. It was the smallest of the three bedrooms, but the mountain was visible from one of the windows.

"This will be great," Melissa said. "I think the rest of my boxes will fit here. You wouldn't think I had accumulated so much stuff. This box," she said, kneeling beside one labeled OUT1-5, "is the first five drafts of *Outerstream*. And this is photographs from conventions and conferences. Look." She held out a picture. "Nina Totenberg and Molly Ivins. They did a talk on women in journalism and I caught them just as they were leaving."

Both women looked rather startled. "I love Molly Ivins," Sarah said, handing back the photograph.

"The photo was used by *Lesbian Lives*. Of course they couldn't pay me, but I did get a credit and they gave me a carte blanche press credential that's been very useful. I cover conferences and events for them and usually can get in free that way."

"You really work hard," Sarah said. "And sometimes for so little reward."

"It's rewarding to see my name in print," Melissa said, looking up from a handful of photographs. "And

I know that someday someone will get a proposal from me and recognize the name from having seen it around, and then I'll be on my way."

"I have complete faith that it will happen someday soon," Sarah said. Melissa's self-confidence was infectious. She liked that Melissa had dreams; she'd had them herself and some of them had come true. "Do you want to empty your car today? Or do it little by little so you can organize?"

"Oh, let's do it now," Melissa said. "The Nova is going to come apart at the seams if I don't get some of the stuff out of it."

They spent the next few hours carrying in boxes and the one suitcase of clothing Melissa possessed. It took a few minutes for her to move her clothes into the drawers and onto the rack and shelves Sarah had emptied for her in the large master bedroom.

The boxes were stacked two deep and five high along one wall of the room Melissa proudly called her office. "There's plenty of room left for a desk and a chair and then I can set up my computer and get going."

"I have a card table in the garage until you find a desk you like."

"A card table is all the desk I need." She turned suddenly and fixed Sarah with her silver gaze. "I — this is the right thing for me, I can tell. I'm feeling really creative and happy. Thank you."

"You're welcome," Sarah said. She basked in Melissa's million-dollar smile. "I really want a shower and some food. What do you think?"

"Would that shower be solitaire, or can anyone join in?"

Sarah waggled her eyebrows in answer. The shower took a most predictable and enjoyable turn when Melissa ran her soapy hands over Sarah's shoulders, then turned Sarah to face the spray.

Melissa's hands began a sensuous journey across Sarah's back. "You have a tattoo," she said, sounding surprised.

Sarah smiled into the water. "Mmm-hmmm."

"It's so small I didn't see it before. What do the circles mean?"

"They stand for the five continents," Sarah said, spluttering a little. "I didn't have a lot of time, so I didn't get them in the right colors. And the tattoo guy didn't really get the overlap right, either."

Melissa's tongue flicked across the tattoo and a delightful shiver ran down Sarah's spine. "It's cute. And sexy."

"Makes a strapless gown interesting."

"You, in a strapless gown?"

"Check the closet, I've got three."

"I'd have never said you were *that* femmey." Kisses traced from one shoulder blade to the other.

"I am what I am," Sarah said, turning around.

"What's that?" Melissa twined her fingers in the soft curls between Sarah's legs.

"A woman. Who wants you," Sarah said, drawing Melissa's mouth to hers.

Debra handed over a bottle of California Chardonnay and smiled brightly. "Best behavior, I promise."

Sarah smiled wryly. "I'll believe that when I see it," she said, then led the way to the kitchen where Melissa was tossing the salad. She was gratified to see Debra do a double-take, but found Debra's knowing wink — Debra never made any bones about being a physical being living on a physical plane — annoying. She knew without a doubt that Debra thought she was with Melissa because Melissa was gorgeous.

Dinner went surprisingly well. Debra was at her most charming and irreverent, and after dinner she and Melissa discovered the same disdain for some of the movies in Sarah's video collection. They hollered rude comments from the living room as they rooted around for something to watch while Sarah made cappuccino.

After a few minutes they gave up harassing her and she heard the conversation turn to other topics.

"You really met Martina?" Sarah heard the skepticism in Debra's voice.

"Sure. It was at a reception for the Human Rights Campaign Fund. She's really attractive in person."

"I'll bet," Debra said.

"There's a rumor that she'll be at the Women's Entrepreneur Symposium in Portland in a couple of months. I was thinking of going, but I don't have the airfare . . . or gas money, for that matter. But I might get some bucks from some photos I sent out a few weeks ago. It would be great to see her again."

Debra said again, "I'll bet," and Sarah pursed her lips. It sounded like Debra's best behavior was wearing off.

"I hope you can go," Sarah said as she brought in a tray with large mugs topped with froth and chocolate shavings. "It sounds interesting." It was the first she had heard of the symposium, but she knew that Melissa felt that being in circulation at all sorts of women's events was the only way she would find a forum for her writing, photography and, someday, her film work. She opened her mouth to offer gas money, but Debra interrupted her.

"Sarah met Martina too, didn't you, Sarah?"

Sarah gave Debra her best shut-up-now look. "It's hardly the same thing at all."

Melissa raised her eyebrows. "You could have told me. Here I've been babbling on and on and you could have at least said you knew her."

"I met her. I don't know her," Sarah said. "We exchanged about five words. I believe I said she had played marvelously and she said thank you. That's not 'knowing' somebody."

"You saw her play tennis? Before her career as an activist?"

"Um-hmmm. More pie?" She gestured with the pie tin toward Debra.

Debra shook her head. "Two pieces is my limit." She picked an apple out of the tin and then licked her fingers clean. She sat back with her cappuccino. "This is fabulous," she said, after sipping. "Where was it you met her? Wimbledon? Or the French Open?"

Sarah slapped Debra's hand as she reached for another piece of apple. "I thought you had your limit," she said. "It was the French Open, I don't remember which year."

"Wow," Melissa said. "Are there any other famous dykes you've met and haven't told me about?"

"She's the most famous," Sarah said lightly. "My mother met Eleanor Roosevelt, though."

"Eleanor Roosevelt?" Melissa looked blank. "Oh, the Lorena Hickok thing. I wouldn't say she was a real lesbian."

"Neither would she," Debra said. "But they did

share a bed whenever they could and Eleanor was probably not in Franklin's after he fell in love with what's-her-name."

"Her life is not really the typical lesbian one," Melissa said.

"What is a typical lesbian life?" Debra reached for the pie tin, gave Sarah a peevish look and instead licked at the whipped cream on her cappuccino.

"Well, most lesbians do not become the First Lady."

"You got me there," Debra said.

Melissa smiled sweetly. "And most lesbians are not really in the mainstream. They're struggling, confronting homophobia every day. Trying to express themselves."

Debra blinked. "Well, I've always thought that we were ten percent of every type of woman. I suppose that means that there are a few lesbians in the Christian Coalition."

"They aren't real lesbians," Melissa said. "I firmly believe that a lesbian who hasn't come out of the closet isn't really a lesbian yet."

Debra frowned. "I'll admit that there is a profound life change when a woman comes out of the closet, but she was a lesbian before she took that step or she would never have *had* to come out of the closet."

Sarah interjected, "Debra's a litigator, it doesn't pay to argue with her. She majored in sophistry."

Melissa bit back whatever it was she had been going to say and looked down at her mug instead.

Debra swatted Sarah's arm. "Are there any more of those little cookies?"

"Does your sweet tooth ever quit?"

They wrangled like the good friends they were even though Sarah was miffed by Debra's increasingly patronizing tone with Melissa. She obviously didn't take her seriously. Yes, Melissa was young, just starting out on a career, but Sarah hadn't wanted to crush her enthusiasm by mentioning that she too had met some famous lesbians and non-lesbians in her time.

In my time, she thought. It sounded like her life is over. Like the most exciting part was behind her. There *had* been a lot of excitement in the past. She looked at Melissa and felt the familiar thump in her ribs. There was going to be a lot of excitement in the future.

When Debra left they cleaned up in companionable silence. Afterwards they sat down in the living room with small glasses of anisette.

Melissa turned to Sarah with a rueful smile. "Your friend is very nice, but I don't think she liked me much."

"Debra is — Debra. She will definitely grow on you. She's a little high-strung, but she's also loyal ... and thoughtful in her way."

"I'm not ... breaking anything up, am I? A couple of times I thought she was maybe, well, jealous of me."

Sarah frowned slightly. "Well, I guess she might be worried you'll change our friendship, which is probably true, but she's not a shallow person — it won't bother her for long."

"You and she never ...."

"Never." Sarah smiled indulgently. "I told you in Louisville that I'm not a casual person. Debra and I are friends. I don't sleep with my friends."

"Does that mean we're not friends?" Melissa stroked the back of Sarah's hand.

"We're lovers and very soon I hope we'll feel more like friends too. I think it takes friendship to

build a successful relationship. And friendship...
takes a while to build."

"I think you're right," Melissa said. "I've never
stayed in one place for long enough to make friends.
Friendship is harder to build than — you know, I
can't think of a word to describe exactly what we are
at this moment. In lust?"

"Most definitely." She raised Melissa's fingertips
to her lips and nibbled.

"On the verge of friendship?"

"Probably." Sarah tickled Melissa's palm with the
tip of her tongue.

"And maybe just a little bit in love?"

"Indubitably," Sarah said, trying to keep her tone
light. Just thinking of saying "I love you" made her
insides freeze up with panic. But she wanted to say
it. She pulled Melissa's index finger into her mouth,
sucking gently on it and heard Melissa's quickly
drawn-in breath.

"Sarah...how do you do that?"

"Do what?" Sarah turned her attention to
Melissa's thumb.

"Make me so gawdawful horny all at once?"

For an answer, Sarah pulled Melissa down on top
of her and nuzzled intently through Melissa's soft
chambray shirt. She found an erect nipple and took
it between her teeth, making Melissa hiss.

Even though the years of office work had added
some inches to Sarah's waist, she had the lasting
tone of a natural athlete. Melissa was equally physical
in her own way, and she began to struggle against
Sarah's attempt to seduce her. They tumbled off the
sofa onto the soft carpet, each looking for a hold as
Sarah tried to return her attention to Melissa's
breasts.

Only when she heard the tearing sound of her blouse did Sarah realize how fiercely they were straining against each other. She hesitated for a moment and Melissa took advantage of it, pushing Sarah onto her back and pulling up her bra through the torn shirt, then firmly capturing a breast in her mouth with a guttural groan.

Something exploded in Sarah and she felt the early stirrings of orgasm. Until Melissa she hadn't known her breasts were capable of providing so much pleasure. There was something else too. She realized she was taking pleasure from the rough way Melissa was kneeing her legs apart and using one free hand to unzip her slacks.

Melissa made a sound of success and pleasure as her fingertips found wetness. Sarah felt a part of her she hadn't even known was closed surge open and she urged Melissa deeply inside her.

"Is this what you want?"

"Yes," Sarah managed through clenched teeth. She rocked against Melissa for breathless minutes, who returned her mouth to Sarah's half-bared breast. "Yes —"

"Hold on," Melissa murmured.

Sarah stiffened against Melissa's thrusts, meeting strength for strength until she could take no more, and she collapsed with a weak cry.

Melissa pulled Sarah's pants all the way off and buried her mouth where Sarah so badly needed her. Sarah found herself helplessly crying even as orgasm finally swept through her.

"Darling," she heard Melissa whispering. "Don't cry. Jesus, don't cry."

Sarah struggled to control her sobbing as Melissa held her. When she could she excused herself to find a tissue and throw some cold water on her face. A few minutes later she heard Melissa come to the bathroom door.

"Are you okay?"

"Yes," Sarah said. "I don't know where that came from, but I'm pretty sure it was because I liked it."

"I wasn't too rough with you?"

"No. That wasn't it. I mean, I liked it, but that's not why I cried. I haven't felt that connected to anybody in a long time. If ever. Like you knew what I needed before I thought it."

"I'm flattered," Melissa said slowly. "But, I don't know how to say this, but the women you were with before — did they know?"

"Know what I needed? I thought they did." One of the givens in her relationship with Jane had been that Sarah unusually initiated sex, and it was Jane, the non-athlete, who spent most of the time on her back. At the time, the control Jane had given her had been erotic, but their relationship had withered when Sarah realized she no longer wanted the role. "I thought I knew. But there's never been anyone like you."

"And no one like you," Melissa said softly. "I was having a lot of encounters with politics in bed instead of good sex, you know what I mean?"

Sarah shook her head and padded out to the bedroom. Melissa followed her and together they turned back the covers on the king-sized bed.

"I'll give you an example. There was this woman, Elaine, and she and I hit it off right away and we were in bed and everything was going really well, I thought, until I flipped her over and tried to lean over her. She freaked. She said I was trying to top her and role-playing was patriarchal and I was just acting out violence against women."

Sarah felt a laugh bubble up. She was feeling giddy and lightheaded. She slipped between the sheets and made room for Melissa.

Melissa continued, her tone wry, "That's what I did — I laughed. She threw me out. Unfortunately, she then proceeded to tell everyone else at the seminar I was into sadism. And all I did was flip her on her back."

"Maybe she was a turtle in another life."

Melissa chuckled and hugged her. "You are feeling better, aren't you?"

Sarah nodded. "What other kinds of politics have you run into?"

"Oh, there was the woman who didn't want to fuck because it aped male-female eroticism, and another who thought that my attention to her breasts was based on male objectification of her body."

"I'm glad you objectify me," Sarah said.

"But there's no one like you. You seem to know what I want too."

Sarah struggled to sit upright. "You really wiped me out. I couldn't —"

"That's not what I want," Melissa said in a low tone. She reached over and turned out the lights. "I want you to hold me, and kiss me, and then I want your mouth on me . . ."

The rest was lost in the featherlight kiss Sarah gave her and the soft sound of their mutual sigh.

The next six weeks were heaven for Sarah. Since Melissa's car was lucky to make it to the grocery store, three days out of five she drove Sarah to work so she could run errands or go to appointments. There wasn't a lesbian or gay community group or arts organization that she hadn't visited, met with the heads of or written to, if phone numbers weren't available.

Sarah arrived at her desk every day with the energy of ten patent attorneys and plowed through her work at a rate that raised her boss's eyebrows. She even began the map of the next application after the one she was working on and sent detailed memos to the software engineers about the timing of the specifications. She reiterated the need for unique elements to claim a patentright, as opposed to a copyright, and asked the engineers to let her know which approach would be needed for the new software. They'd told her it was "unique," but all software engineers thought their tweaked version of Tetris was unique. Only one version could get the patent. A few hours later, she got an e-mail back from the engineers telling her not to get her knickers in a twist. Typical.

Debra remained somewhat aloof, but that could have been Sarah's imagination. Debra was preparing for trial in a copyright infringement case, a process so nerve-wracking that Sarah had eschewed it forever. There were too many variables in court and the pace in a civil trial was so slow that she'd found it impossible to test the wind and sight the target.

At night she was usually home by seven, or Melissa would pick her up at the office and they would sample yet another of Seattle's many restaurants. The weeks seemed filled with Alaskan salmon and Vietnamese fish stew and pad thai with shrimp and, of course, lovemaking that never seemed to stop, flowing from one day to the next, from a glance over dinner to a feverish encounter during morning showers.

Sarah could only hope that Melissa was as happy

as she was. She assured Sarah that she was, but Sarah was beginning to realize that as hard as Melissa worked at getting to know people and sending out queries and photo sheets, the response back was slow, and without any firm promises. She could only try to understand how frustrating that must be. What Melissa was trying to do wasn't as easy as hitting a target from 77 yards with a 1/4-inch-thick arrow. The arrow flew, it hit center or it didn't, and that was the kind of instant feedback Sarah understood.

They entered the house one evening on the glow of Seattle Bonvivant curry and orange roughy and a mellow Zinfandel. Without speaking, they bypassed the television and slid into bed with soft laughter, quickly supplanted by more fevered exchanges. As always, Sarah found herself slipping into sleep not long afterward, knowing Melissa was likely to get up to write or watch the news.

It was almost 5 a.m. when Sarah stirred and realized that Melissa was not yet in bed. She wrapped herself in her robe and went in search of her lover.

She wasn't prepared for the tear-streaked face that turned to her when she entered the dimly lit kitchen. Melissa was smoothing a letter under one hand. Other bills and junk mail lay on the table unopened. Sarah felt a chill in her stomach and she sat down next to Melissa and took the nervously fluttering hand in her own.

"Bad news?"

Melissa shook her head. "Good news. I've been thinking. And wondering what to do. I should be jumping for joy." She wiped away a tear.

"Can I read it?" Melissa handed the letter over and Sarah quickly scanned the lines. "But this is fabulous," she said. "A grant to produce your documentary ... oh." She read the final sentences again. Her heart pounded with each word.

> ... While we understand that your scope is to eventually be national, our funds can only be used for research, filming and for the services of crafts- people and artisans all located in the San Francisco area. Your estimate for a smaller scope production based in a single city was approximately $17,000. Our grant of $22,500 should help defray your living expenses during the five to six months you will be residing in this area. If this production meets our expectations, further funding may be available for additional work in the Bay Area.

I should have known, Sarah thought. I should have known this couldn't last. Essentially, Melissa had a job offer — a good one that could catapult her to the prominence she so assiduously sought — and that meant she had to move. The house had been so full since she had arrived. And now it would be empty again. Everything would be empty again because it would take a two-hour flight plus ground time to get to Melissa, and the same amount of time to come home again. She set the letter down carefully and turned to the kitchen window.

Mt. Snoqualmie was limned with a thin line of gold, and then the first shaft of morning light beamed into the valley.

"You should go," Sarah said. "Of course you have to take it."

"I don't want to leave you," Melissa said in a low voice. "I don't know if I can."

"You have to take it," Sarah repeated. "You have

to." She flipped on the coffeemaker and then found herself padding out to the garage. The icy cement bit through her slippers, but she didn't really notice. She opened the case at the end, gathered what she needed and slipped out into the backyard. She walked over the frosted grass and unzipped the tarp covering the target.

Within a few moments she had loaded her quiver, strung her competition bow and nocked her first arrow.

Shhhhhhhwoshhhh-ipppp.

It didn't even make the distance to the target. She cursed softly and nocked again.

The sound of the arrow flying was like a balm to Sarah's shattered spirits. The next five arrows found the target in the red ring, then she planted the next two neatly in the gold. Not bad for someone as badly out of practice as she was.

Grannie MacNeil had said that when two hundred Welsh archers had let fly from the foot of Eyri, the Normans had fallen back, screaming at what they thought were the wings of demons. The air beat with the passage of thousands of arrows in a few short minutes, and the archers of Wales did not miss.

Her solitary arrow flying the length of her long backyard to thump firmly into the target was an echo of finer days, when dreams sometimes came true.

She stopped when her back shrieked for a break, recovered her arrows and slipped the waterproof tarp back over the target. Her slippers were soaking and she could hardly feel her toes.

Inside, she heard the shower running and poured herself a cup of coffee. She tried to be philosophical. You couldn't trust in anything but the sunrise, Grannie had said. The sunrise and yourself. But Sarah had also learned to trust the path of the arrow. Even though she fought them, she felt tears building. The path of the arrow had not taken her to the bulls-eye once again. With Melissa she had discovered she could be the arrow, but now the target was moving.

There was only one way to keep to the path she hoped would bring her the lasting love she longed for. She hung her bathrobe on the back of the bathroom door and joined Melissa in the steamy shower. Melissa greeted her with red-rimmed eyes and exclaimed over Sarah's cold-reddened face, hands and feet.

"Whatever were you doing?" She swung Sarah under the hot spray.

"I'm going with you," Sarah said. Melissa stared at her. "I'm going with you," she repeated, and she pulled Melissa under the hot water for a kiss of promise.

Leslie

MOTION (mo′shen)
[Middle English *mocioun,* from Old French
motion, from Latin *motio, motion-,* from
motus, past participle of *movêre,* to move]
motion (noun); motioned, motioning, motions
(verb, transitive); motion (verb)

1. The act or process of changing position or
   place.
2. A meaningful or expressive change in the
   position of the body or a part of the body;
   a gesture.
3. The ability or power to move.
4. A prompting from within; an impulse or
   inclination.

4

*Desire is moved with violent motion . . . and is
called love. (Socrates)*

"I want proof your homework is done or I'm
pulling the plug." Leslie hovered her index finger
over the main power switch and looked Matt in the
eye.

"Aw, Mom," he said, not unexpectedly.

"Your report card is not what either of us expect
from you. So, from now on, you show me your
finished homework or no computer games. You know
I can set up a password if I have to. Don't make
me."

He kicked the leg of the desk, also not
unexpectedly, then slunk off to his bedroom to get
his books. Leslie sighed. Another eight months of the
terrible twelves. Then it's the terrible thirteens for a
whole year. And so on.

Matt wouldn't be slacking off on his homework if he weren't bright enough to pull in Bs without studying. But Leslie had vowed that she'd stamp out any "good enough to pass" sentiments her son might have. In the scheme of world history, this was not the time to be a lazy white boy.

"Read it aloud to me," Leslie said, when she suspected that Matt was daydreaming and turning pages to make her think he was reading. "I don't know anything about Pierce or Taylor. When I took U.S. History we jumped from war to war and in between is a vague blur."

Leslie half-listened as she finished the dinner dishes. She wiped down the counters and made a short To Do list for the morning. If she was going to have this enforced vacation, she might as well make the most of it. She heard Matt end the chapter and offered him his dessert, but he wrinkled his nose.

"Can I go outside for a while? I know it's getting dark, but I'll stay in the backyard."

"Sure. Fresh air helps the brain."

Matt gave her a look that said, "Yeah, right" and slunk out the back door. She watched his silhouette kick at imaginary rocks.

"Poor little guy," she said to herself. It had been bad enough when his father had moved with Matt's two half-brothers to the East Coast. Instead of seeing his dad every other weekend, or more frequently, he saw him every other 3-week school break in the year-round school schedule.

Then his best friend's mother had gotten a promotion and they had moved to Sacramento. The two boys e-mailed each other, but Matt's evenings and weekends were essentially empty. Leslie knew

how he felt — she missed Carol's coffee cake and
bright wit as much as he missed Lenny's skateboarding and Nintendo.

She could always fill up the hours she'd spent
yakking with Carol with work. The product launch
was looking to happen in about eighteen months and
she was increasingly busy. But Matt needed her more
now than ever.

She tore up her To Do list. "Hey, kiddo," she
called.

"Yeah," floated back out of the darkness.

"Want to go to Great America tomorrow? I
promise not to scream if you go on the Drop Zone,
and I'll write an excuse to the Vice Principal."

"Okay," Matt said from the doorway. "How long
is Uncle Richard going to keep you from going to
work?"

"Well, if everything goes well, they'll let me back
in on Monday."

There was a thump from the front door and
through the screen she heard Richard say, "We'll let
you back in tomorrow."

Leslie flew to the door, unlocked the screen and
dragged Richard into the kitchen. He had a bag full
of hot bagels and what looked like real cream cheese
from the deli at the bottom of the hill. Leslie let out
a high-pitched squeal she hadn't known she was still
capable of and threw her arms around him.

"It works!" They rocked back and forth in each
other's arms, and then Matt bounded into their celebratory hug, adding his own shrill, "It works! It
works!" to the noise.

Matt broke out peach Snapples for all three of
them, while Leslie slathered a steaming pumpernickel

bagel with cream cheese and pressed it to Richard's. "Cheers," she said. Richard was right as always: hot bread and cheese were better than champagne.

"Dammit, Leslie, I'm telling you, it worked the first time we ran it. I'm sorry you missed it." Richard had cream cheese in his mustache and beard.

"Wasn't my idea," Leslie reminded him. She had wanted to watch the first run of the software, but instead had been banished.

"You were making me nervous with all your what-ifs. And the programmers didn't want to screw up in front of you. You're practically their mom."

"Thanks," she said wryly. Some of the programmers at MagicWorks were in their thirties, not that you'd know it from their behavior.

"Uncle Richard, I still don't understand what you and Mom are making," Matt said. Leslie was glad to see that his aura of gloom had lifted considerably.

"Let me give you an example," he said. "Remember in Aladdin how Robin Williams did the voice of the genie?" Matt nodded. "Well, he also inspired the artists who drew the genie. He moved in ways that fit his voice and artists laboriously recorded the gestures and movements. Now imagine if they could have filmed Robin Williams instead. And then matched, say, six to ten of his movements to an equal number of poses for the genie, and then had a computer review all of Robin's performance and then draw all of the genie's movements to match?"

"Uh-huh," Matt said dubiously. "So what does that do?"

"It means quality animation based on human movement without frame-by-frame drawing. It'll be a brand new way to create animated films.

"Think of this, Matt. You could collect some pictures of Abraham Lincoln and scan them into your

78

computer. Then you could film yourself walking and talking, then overlay the pictures of Lincoln and your film and presto! An animated Lincoln that you created based on what you read and knew about him."

"That would be way cool," Matt said. "I could make Lincoln say anything." He bit into his bagel before Leslie noticed the cream cheese was two inches thick.

Leslie met Richard's gaze over Matt's head. They both knew that Matt was likely to create a Lincoln who skateboarded and quoted X-Man.

"Not unimportantly," Richard said, "some very large companies will pay us a great deal to have the software — that is, after your mom finishes convincing them they can't survive without it."

"And no one beats us to it," Leslie added.

"Ever the optimist," Richard said. "So you'll be back at the office bright and early, going through all those résumés you got from prospective attorneys."

Leslie saw Matt's face fall back into his lines of gloom. "Sorry, Richard, but I have plans. Matt's going to play hooky with me." She was rewarded by Matt's first genuine smile in what seemed like weeks.

Richard smiled indulgently. "Fair enough," he said, patting her hand. "Go have fun wherever it is you're going."

"You're a great boss," Leslie told him as he was leaving. "And a great friend."

He kissed her lightly, his attitude fatherly, though at 41 he was only her senior by two years.

"Did Uncle Richard ever want to marry you?" Matt asked the question later that evening from the depths of the pajama top he was pulling over his head.

"Nope, never. We're just best friends," Leslie said.

"We've made great partners for holy moley — twenty years — but romance has never been a part of it. Not like with your dad."

Matt was silent, his face carefully neutral. She knew he was desperately missing his father and thinking about how nice it would have been to have "uncle" Richard around all the time. He understood that she was not interested in men, but at the moment Uncle Richard was the only other adult prominently in her life. Poor little guy, she thought, he was so lonely sometimes, and she knew his loneliness was not a commentary on her mothering. He was just at an age when he wanted . . . more.

He went off to bed and Leslie spent the next hour polishing off another bagel and channel-surfing while she played "if onlies" in her head.

If only she had been happy married to Alan. If only Sharon had been able to adapt to having a kid around, then Matt would have had a second adult in his life on an everyday basis and not miss his dad so much. If only she and Carol had had some flickering of passion between them — they'd have made both their sons ecstatic. If only almost-forty women with offspring didn't produce anti-endorphins in every eligible lesbian they met. If only Captain Janeway would beam into her living room.

She would have moped for a couple more hours, but she remembered that she did have a vastly more interesting job ahead of her, now that they knew their software could work. She needed to start interviewing consultants for package design and technical writing. Her trip to Chicago and New York to interview design agencies was definitely on. And, heaven forbid, she had to hire a lawyer to write their patent application and take care of a lot of other corporate business Leslie didn't even want to think about. Maybe she could get Richard to do the dirty deed. She'd had an antipathy for lawyers ever since they had almost turned her amicable divorce from Allan into World War III.

It was going to be fun interviewing graphics firms and ad agencies, and playing with design and marketing literature. Let Richard hire the lawyer.

"So, Geoff, I have a favor to ask," Sarah said. "I'm moving to your neck of the woods —"

"You are? This is a great place to live. You'll love it here. Why are you pulling up your stakes?"

"Remember my paramour in Louisville?" Sarah shoved down the little flutter in her heart. Romance was singing "I Will Follow Him" with the appropriate change of pronoun.

"How could I forget? I hardly saw you after she showed up."

"Well, she has this really great opportunity to produce a documentary, but she has to move to the Bay Area to do it, and the idea of commuting back and forth to see her is just too much for me."

"You are *that* besotted? She must be a real Circe." Geoff sounded skeptical.

"Besotted doesn't cover it," Sarah said. "We've been living together for almost two months and I still don't see enough of her."

"Sounds faintly nauseating," Geoff said. "So what's this favor you need?"

"I bet there's a local job bulletin from your AAPA chapter you could fax me . . ."

"There is indeed. I have it right here. The only

thing of interest is a software start-up company, and I'd apply but the paycheck would be a cut for me. I can't live on promises of huge bonuses when the software takes off."

"Oh," Sarah said, trying not to let her disappointment show. "Basically, in lieu of partial pay you become a part investor, so to speak."

"You got it. Of course I know someone who did that with Netscape and now he has a cabin in Vail and a yacht in the Bahamas."

Sarah piffed. "I should be so lucky. But I guess a lead is better than arriving with no place to interview. Can you fax the ad to me? Send it to my home fax, because my boss knows I'm leaving, but no one else does yet." She rattled off the number. "You're a doll," she added.

"I know. It's going to be great having you in this part of the world. I don't think I know anyone who dances as well as you do."

"Except you, kind sir," Sarah teased.

"You'll have to let me parade you at the company Christmas party. We will cut an impressive figure."

"I don't suppose Melissa will mind," Sarah said. "She's going to be very busy, and she doesn't particularly like dancing. And if I don't find a job right away, I'm going to have a lot of time on my hands."

Geoff's speaker beeped and he hurriedly said good-bye. Sarah sat staring at the phone for a few minutes. Romance was still singing "I Will Follow Him," but she was sure she could hear another voice crooning, "Bewitched, Bothered and Bewildered."

"Listen, Matt, I don't have time to argue with you about it. Start laying out the stuff you want to take with you and we'll discuss this when I get home. I've got a million things to do."

"Aw, Mom," was Matt's answer, but he hung up and Leslie turned her attention back to her desk.

"Les, I wanted to give you this before you go." She looked up, then waved Mark Davis into a chair. "It's the time specs and, well, I wrote some ideas I have for marketing, and I have a name I kind of like."

Leslie hid her sigh of irritation. "Mark, everyone has ideas and I'm glad to consider them. But —"

"I know, I'm just a programmer and all my creativity comes out in C Plus Plus or not at all."

"That's not what I meant. Yes, it is. That *is* what I meant," Leslie admitted. "I'm sorry, Mark. I've been deluged with input today."

"Well, unlike all the other geeks who work here, I wrote my ideas down. In English, not code." He handed her a neatly stapled document no more than a few pages long.

"You're the king," Leslie said, making her voice breathy. She fluttered her eyelashes. "The master. The absolute best programmer who works here —" A cough from the doorway made her look up. "The best programmer sitting in my office," she hastily amended. "What can I do for you, Gene?"

Mark excused himself, murmuring something politic about getting back to work. Gene Williams eased himself into the chair Mark had vacated and swallowed a long slug from his Jolt cola.

"I told the guys to leave you alone today," Gene said. "But you've still had a steady stream of them. Sorry about that."

"It's okay. They're all so excited about the product and don't realize that I'm not making any decisions about the way we package it on this trip. I want to get ideas from the agencies. And it's not as if we're rolling out for mass market like we did with MagicBullet."

"I know," Gene said. At thirty-seven, he was the managing programmer, and the oldest of the bunch. "But since I'm here —"

Leslie laughed. "Go ahead, give me your ideas."

"Actually, I don't have any. But I read Mark's stuff while it was in the printer tray, and he's got a very hot idea for the name."

Leslie flipped through the pages, then cocked her head to one side. "Motion." She mimicked tasting wine. "I like it. I'll play with it," she promised. "You can tell Mark I liked it. It's certainly better than Piglet."

"Hey, no one told you we renamed it now that it works, did they? Piglet is still the code name for all the prototypes, but what we're working on now is called Tigger." He launched into the Tigger song and wouldn't stop until Leslie pushed him out of her office.

She leaned out of her door, looking for Melody, the secretary/administrative assistant extraordinaire she and Richard shared. No sign of her as usual. Lord knows she had become the fastest typist Leslie had ever seen, but she balanced it nicely against a propensity to gossip and undertake duties nowhere near her job description, like restocking the fridge in the programmers' cave of a work area. She suspected that Melody had followed Mark back to the cave with plans to hibernate.

Richard's door was ajar, so she peeked in and found him hunched over his keyboard.

"Hey boss, I'm almost out of here," she said.

He grunted and continued typing, then looked up. "I found us an attorney," he said.

"You already went through the stack I sorted for you?"

He shook his head. "This one came in the fax this morning." He waved a piece of paper in her direction, so she had no option but to take it.

"But what about —"

"I have a good feeling about this one."

Leslie bit back an exasperated sigh. Richard could be so maddening. If she argued with him he'd never look at the others. She glanced down at the résumé in her hand.

"Well, she seems pretty qualified. CompuSoft? Richard, I thought you said we'd never hire anyone from the home of computer fascism."

"Ah, but this fascist is abandoning ship."

"After what, six years? I hardly think it's for ideological reasons after this long."

"I have a good feeling," he said again, and then he gave her one of the smiles that made her fillings ache. The smile said, "I've made up my mind and all further discussion is to humor you."

"Will you at least look at the top six résumés in the stack? They're just as qualified and maybe one of them will give you a feeling, too. You never know, this MacNeil woman could give you hives when you actually interview her and you'll need a second choice."

"I'll look them over," he promised.

"Jesus H., Richard. Is this your little lesson in what happens when Leslie delegates upward?"

He smiled again and Leslie just kept herself from stamping her foot. He could bring out the child in her so easily, the brat. Smiling as sweetly as she could manage, she put the MacNeil woman's résumé back on his desk.

"I'll see you in two weeks," she said.

He waved and went on smiling.

Brat.

"Knock 'em dead, baby," Melissa said, then she kissed Sarah breathlessly. "I know you'll be great. They'll beg you to work for them."

Sarah returned the breathless kiss with a more thorough one of her own, then she slid out of the Jaguar in front of Pacific Air. She waved to Melissa as she drove away, then watched the car until it was out of sight. Melissa was bound for the symposium in Portland — Sarah had convinced her that it was foolish to pass up the chance to network when it was only a long day's drive away.

Besides, she was going to be in San Francisco for half the time Melissa would be gone, so why shouldn't Melissa go? Faced with such logic, Melissa had conceded with a loving kiss. Sarah strode through the terminal with her overnight bag bouncing on one hip and knew she was smiling. All she had to do was think of their future and the smiles wouldn't stop. She founding herself humming "For Once in My Life." Debra had given up on her and while Sarah regretted the loss of closeness with Debra, she couldn't let it dim her happiness and a sense of well-being that she hoped would carry her through what was sure to be an unusual interview.

Sarah supposed it was a good sign of MagicWorks's solvency that they were willing to pop for her airfare. Richard Deacon was a character, that was for sure. He'd been quite anxious to meet with her right away and assured her a Saturday appointment was no problem. It was almost as if he had a deadline to meet. But he was the president, and they make their own deadlines. Usually. He'd also mentioned that there was a lot of negotiating room in the salary, and if it came to nothing she'd still have the weekend in San Francisco where she could access Alumni Resources for more career opportunities and look for a place to live.

The fog was just lifting in San Francisco as they made the final approach, and the pilot even dipped the wing on the right side of the plane to give them all a better look at the unforgettable landscape. Two beautiful bridges, green islands, ridges encrusted with eucalyptus, a gigantic park right off the ocean and a thick forest to the north... Sarah's spirits soared. She would love living in this city, as much as she loved Seattle. There were hiking trails and redwoods close by, perhaps not as magnificent as Olympic Forest and Mt. Rainier, but the green was there, in sustaining abundance. She already knew that there was a thriving archery community and she might run into a few familiar faces.

As she navigated the compact rental car from the airport in South San Francisco to Mountain View, her spirits dipped a little. From the highway it all looked like one big strip mall. They drooped further when her destination appeared to be an industrial park that had seen better days. But the green and blue MagicWorks logo was not as dilapidated as the building it was attached to.

The side door was unlocked as Richard had promised and she thought it was bad security. But the moment she stepped inside she was greeted by a bright-eyed young woman whose every move was accompanied by a faint tinkling sound... coming from the small bells at the ends of her corn row braids.

"You must be Sarah MacNeil," she said with a

welcoming smile. "I'm Melody Baker. I'm thrilled to meet you. I've never met an Olympian before, although my brother was an NCAA finalist in discus one year, but he tore a ligament, you know this one right here —" She pointed to her elbow. "And that was that, but he probably never would have made it to the Games, but you did twice, and you even —"

"Thanks for watching the door, Melody."

Sarah turned to face the newcomer. "You must be Richard Deacon." She fought down a smile. He reminded her of a rather short department store Santa Claus, except he was dressed in jeans and a T-shirt left over from a Grateful Dead concert.

"I am indeed. Come right with me and we'll get down to business." His smile of greeting came with a knowing half-wink just like Edmund Gwynn's in *Miracle on 34th Street.* Sarah suspected he was a charmer, which meant he could also be . . . difficult.

Sarah smiled thanks at Melody, who seemed rather nice if you liked bubbly personalities.

"Yes, she's always that way," Richard said, once again as if he knew what Sarah was thinking. "I wouldn't have her any other way. But then, I'm a morning person."

"So am I," Sarah said. "I have colleagues who think I should be skinned at those wonderful eight-thirty staff meetings." She felt her back muscles relax.

"Can I get you some coffee?"

"No, thanks. The one thing airlines give you these days is coffee and I'm all coffeed out for the day."

"Hungry?" He glanced at his watch. "Geez, it's after lunch." He punched a button on his phone. "Melody, are there any sandwiches left?"

"I think so," came the answer. "You want one?

How about Ms. MacNeil? I think there's two turkey with Swiss."

Richard was so obviously hungry that Sarah nodded when he glanced at her inquiringly. Truth be told, she was starving, but eating and answering questions was not the easiest thing to do gracefully.

Melody popped in a few moments later with two sandwiches, a small bag of Fritos and two sodas. She handed the Jolt cola to Richard and proffered the other can to Sarah.

"I pegged you for a Diet Coke kind of woman," Melody said.

"You pegged me right." Sarah took the can with a smile and found herself thinking she could get used to working with these people.

Richard took an enormous bite out of his sandwich. After a swallow, he observed, "You don't look like a CompuSoft fascist."

Sarah choked on her sandwich. "Just what does a CompuSoft fascist look like?"

"Sweaters," Richard said, grinning. "Sweaters and vests."

Sarah glanced down at her dove gray suit. "I do own sweaters. I want to be clear on that point."

"I forgive you," Richard said with a broad grin. More soberly, he said, "Look, Sarah, I can't describe our product to you unless you come on board and sign all that stuff our outside counsel recommends, and you can't talk about what exactly you're working on, I'll bet."

Sarah nodded. Her confidentiality agreement with CompuSoft was iron-clad.

"So why don't we talk about the current status of copyrighting and patenting software. General terms."

"Sure," Sarah said. She launched into a synopsis

of her current understanding of the increasing difficulty of patenting software. She finished with, "Even if we can convince the patent office that our product is unique right down to what it produces, they still have the option not to review the application. If they do decide to review it, they can turn it down up until three years later. So I think it's worthwhile to apply for a patent, but we should copyright every word of the code and protect ourselves with the usual trade and service marks for the product."

"I'm learning more every minute," Richard said. "We never bothered to do anything about MagicBullet and no one ever infringed on it."

Sarah swallowed her last bite of the sandwich. "Well, the most likely explanation for that is who would want to infringe on it? You made a sensible, inexpensive product almost every PC user has and there's no room for profit to anyone else. I mean, you still sell it for what . . . eight bucks? Who would want to cut in on that? You saturated your market in just a few months because you made it available online. I'm guessing that what you're working on now is something a great deal more complicated and expensive. So there will be people who would like to come out with their own discounted version of your software. They'll plan their own release at just the right time . . . after *you* spend the money educating the users about why they need it. Then they'll compete based on price and clean up."

Richard wrinkled his nose. "I know people do business that way. Still disappointing, but there we are. Okay, you've convinced me we do need an attorney for this process. Why would I need you as opposed to these —" he waved his hand at a stack of résumés on his desk — "eminently qualified people?

Well, some of them are qualified. Or so I've been told." For a moment he looked as if he'd been caught saying too much.

"I've been through the whole process, from start to finish. I was assistant on the patent process for CompuSoft's DOS add-on operating system, and I've been the lead or solo attorney for the last three years for a number of their home entertainment products."

"Including virtual reality, multimedia and video synthesis?"

Sarah nodded. "I can also offer you my expertise at inside security. As you get closer to a final product you'll need to tighten up control on the programmers."

"They'll love that," Richard said.

"I've been the heavy before," Sarah said with a shrug. "I've learned to live without the love of programmers, but I usually manage to win their respect."

"When could you start?"

The question caught Sarah off guard. "Are you offering me the position?"

"I don't like to beat around the bush. I follow my intuition and my intuition says you'll work out fine. Everyone will like working with you, including the . . . marketing person. I'd introduce you but she's on a business trip."

"We would need to talk about salary before I'd commit myself."

Richard smiled. "Of course. Well, as I said, the salary is negotiable. We can also sweeten the pot with stock that could be worth something some day. No guarantees."

Sarah chuckled because he so obviously meant her to, but she could sense that the future of the company was no laughing matter to him. "You've been very honest with me. It's bad negotiating tactics, did you know that? At least that's what I learned in law school."

"I'm not sure I subscribe to that theory."

"Well, if I'm going to work for you, I should probably adopt some of your methods," Sarah said, trying to hide a smile that kept threatening what should be a serious moment in the interview. "I'm moving here for personal reasons and I have no other sure leads. And I'm beginning to think that maybe I wouldn't mind a change of working environment."

"You can wear jeans. Not that your suit doesn't . . . ah . . . suit you." Richard gestured at his faded T-shirt. "We're pretty casual. Except when we've got outside meetings."

"I'm used to a lot of latitude in schedule, a private office and something with a Pentium chip in it. But I rarely need secretarial services — I can't think unless I type it."

"The office and hardware is a given. Melody can handle almost anything if you ask nicely. And I'm a real believer in treating people like grown-ups. You know what you need to do. How and when you do it is your business unless it becomes my business. If you know what I mean."

"When can I start?" This time there was no stopping her smile. It felt right.

Richard guffawed. "We haven't talked about money." He offered a sum higher than in the ad and added a hundred shares of stock annually.

Sarah found herself nodding and just like that they struck their deal. She was a little amazed at how easy it was and hoped she didn't get home and have a major attack of the regrets.

They continued talking as they finished the Fritos, then he led her back to the general office area and gave her a hearty handshake and his best wishes for a safe journey home. "If you need a few extra days to get settled before you report, just give me a call. Moving is not an easy business."

"I'll be sure to let you know if that's the case. And I'm looking forward to working with you."

For a moment, Richard looked slightly guilty about something, but his expression resumed its usual benign charm. "The feeling is mutual," he said, then waved cheerily as she walked to her rental car.

She was on the highway headed for San Francisco before the enormity of what she'd just done sank in. She found herself grinning from ear to ear. She switched on the radio and when Patti Labelle's "New Attitude" came on she turned it up loud enough to drown out her own off-key singing. She crested a steep hill and suddenly the panorama of San Francisco spread out before her. The sky was brilliantly blue. The hills were dusty gold. The Golden Gate Bridge winked orange and the deep green bay was studded with gleaming sailboats that scudded across whitecaps.

She would grow to love this place, and she was sure her job would be interesting and rewarding. Though her heart still fluttered over the precipitousness of her decision to move with Melissa, the panic — hammering her in the middle of the night — was more than manageable.

She had hit the bulls-eye.

"You *hired* her? Did you even look at the other résumés?"

Richard's silence told Leslie the answer. He looked distinctly guilty.

"I can't believe this," Leslie said heatedly. "Are you ever going to grow up? You can't just hire someone because you had a feeling she'd work out. You didn't even check her references."

"You'll like her," he said.

"That's not the point," she snapped, sure she would hate this Sarah person on sight. "We need someone to do a bang-up job for us —"

"She'll do that too." He was starting to look faintly amused.

"Richard, you drive me crazy sometimes." It didn't help that Melody had already babbled about the wonder woman they'd hired. Something about her being an athlete, as if that was some sort of credential for being a lawyer.

"Only sometimes?"

"Stop trying to make me laugh. Just because you're the genius behind all of us probably becoming millionaires doesn't give you license to ignore the best advice you can get. Especially mine."

The everpresent smile left his eyes. "Les, you could have had this chair as easily as me. And you know it."

Leslie made a face at her shoes. "How did we get into this, Richie? We don't know what we're doing."

"That's never stopped us before," he reminded her. "Okay, so the organic fruit farm didn't make it. But we had a hell of a lot of fun even if we didn't get rich."

"Getting rich wasn't the point."

"It still isn't. I mean, yes, we've thought of a software concept and so far have picked the right people to help us get it on the market. So what if our original idea was to make an educational tool

94

before we realized Disney or Amblin would kill for it?"

"I still don't know how we got here. Arguing about a stupid lawyer, for God's sake."

"You're the one arguing —" He cut off Leslie's angry splutter with a raised hand. "Okay, I ignored your advice and picked someone because of a feeling. It's the same feeling I had when we hired Gene to manage the programmers. And was I right?"

"You were right," Leslie admitted, sullenly. She realized she sounded like Matt.

"And Melody? I said she would learn to type, but smarts mattered more."

"You were right again. You're always right, Richard. When do I get to be right?" She rolled her eyes. "Forget I said that. You always manage to make me revert to Leslie-the-seventeen-year-old. You haven't changed a bit."

"It wouldn't hurt you to get in touch with the seventeen-year-old you used to be."

"Blah, blah, blah," Leslie said. "Go beat your tom-tom in the woods, Iron Man."

He frowned. "Be serious, Les. At this point in both our lives we need to be real about what we want."

"I want Matt to grow up in a safer world where he can blossom into a happy and genuine human being."

"What do *you* want?"

"I just said it. I'm a mom, now and forever."

"That's not particularly healthy —"

"Richard, how come we're not talking about your decision to flout my advice? Why are we talking about me?"

95

The twinkle came back to his eyes. "You have changed, Les. Ten years ago you'd have chased every red herring I threw at you."

She slapped him on the arm, just hard enough for him to know she sort of meant it. "Bastard."

"Hey, I just wanted to make sure we understood each other . . . about how we feel. And why we're here."

"I'm still pissed at you."

"Okay." He shrugged. "I deserve it. But I think you'll like her. She's a morning person," he added, the gleam in his eye turning wicked.

"Oh, terrific. That's terrific," Leslie said. "I'm going to come to work and find memos on my desk, aren't I? Let me say one thing, Richard Deacon. I'll get even with you."

"I think you always have," he said. His phone buzzed and he waved his cheery good-bye as she stalked out.

Anybody else would have fired her for that tantrum, and she knew it. But she wasn't exactly an employee. She had lost the toss on who would be the president versus vice president. Then Richard had wanted to go best out of three. And he'd won again. Best of five and three beers later — still Richard. He really hadn't wanted to be in charge but fate was fate, they'd decided. Most of the time he wasn't the boss — he was too busy reviewing programming to worry about the details of running the rest of the company.

Why, oh why hadn't she just buckled down and hired the attorney herself? As she walked by what would be Sarah MacNeil's office, she saw that Melody had already cleaned the desk vacated over two years ago by their last shipping manager. Online delivery of software had eliminated the need, but as was their philosophy, they hadn't eliminated any personnel except by attrition. A new computer had been set up, and Melody had put a MagicWorks mug next to the phone. Leslie sighed loudly and realized that she sounded just like Matt.

5

Your embraces alone give life to my heart.
(Unknown)

"What on earth is that?" Melissa pointed at the tall, thin, leather pouch Sarah had pulled from the back of the bedroom closet.

"My longbow," Sarah said, feeling shy. She was uneasily aware that she hadn't ever talked to Melissa about what archery had meant to her, and what she'd achieved when she'd been actively shooting. She put her reluctance down to not wanting to parade her accomplishments in front of someone so desperately seeking her own glories. She didn't want any element of competitiveness in their relationship. "I'll show you."

She unzipped the pouch and drew out the five-foot, seven-inch bow, exactly one inch shorter than she was. She quickly strung it and realized that it wasn't as easy as it had been five years ago. Not enough practice. And too much sitting in an office. She nocked a phantom arrow onto the taut string and drew the string back. Her fingers screamed at the lack of tabs to protect them from almost fifty pounds of draw weight, but she drew fully.

"Sight." She drew down on an orange in her favorite Cezanne print. "Focus." Her fingers released the string gratefully and the thrum filled her ears like a love song. "Fly." With an arrow at this range, the orange would have become a neat hole with an arrow sunk to its fletchings. This bow was capable of almost twice the distance of a standard competition bow.

"You don't do those war games in the woods, do you?"

Sarah flushed. "Of course not. It's not something to play with. This bow can be deadly from four hundred feet. At close range it will do more damage than a rifle."

"Eewww." Melissa's delicate nose wrinkled. "It's too violent for me."

Violent? Sarah had never found the magic of the bow in her hands violent. Of course her forebears had gone to war with bows and had killed other men. Grannie MacNeil had hunted with her bow in the Cascades. Sarah's favorite Christmas dinner memory was replete with wild goose. Her father had been proud of his mother's prowess at both hunting and cooking, but Sarah remembered that her own mother had been fastidiously repelled.

When Sarah had first shown interest in archery, her mother had said it wasn't ladylike. By then her parents were divorced and her father sent Sarah off to Grannie MacNeil's every summer where she'd learned to pickle cucumbers, can peaches, pluck

chickens and draw a bow. Grannie said she'd teach
Sarah to hunt but made it plain that if she shot
anything she'd have to do the rendering and cleaning
herself. Her city-bred twelve-year-old stomach hadn't
been up to the idea, so her practice had always been
target shooting. She'd been proud of the calluses on
her fingertips, but her mother had been appalled
come the fall.

Those calluses had almost gone away.

"Are you going to stand there all day?"

Sarah turned to Melissa, wanting to explain about
Grannie MacNeil and the years she'd spent perfecting
her stance, learning to sense the wind against her
face, handling pressure and ignoring judges and
crowds. But Melissa was already pulling open another
box.

"Do you think I should clean this out a little
before I pack it," she said, holding up a thick sheaf
of papers. "Come look. These are my first photos."

Sarah slipped Grannie MacNeil's bow back into its
pouch and set it carefully next to the boxes
containing her past.

"I wish the apartment had more storage," Melissa
said.

"There's space," Sarah said. "We'll just have to be
judicious about what we keep in the apartment, and
put the rest in storage." Accepting the job at
MagicWorks had left her with the weekend to find a
place for them to live. The rent had been far more
than she had expected — almost as much as she'd
have paid for one of the hillside apartments near
Pike's Market with a heartstopping view of the
Sound. She had lucked out finding something that
was near the Castro district — Melissa's only
stipulation. It had two bedrooms and a large, airy

living room looking down on the Castro Theater several blocks down the hill.

Beyond the neon theater sign the Financial District rose into view, with black, brown, gray and white skyscrapers reaching for a sky that had been powder blue when she'd last seen it. The view had been a necessity for her own sanity—she couldn't go from Mt. Snoqualmie to someone else's wall. She expected that eventually she'd sell the house and buy something in the Bay Area, but she wanted to get to know the area before making a decision that big.

In the meantime, Debra, who reminded Sarah daily that she really wasn't speaking to her, said she wanted to rent Sarah's house. She had phrased it more like, "I'd love to live there until you come to your senses." Debra had an aversion to owning things and she liked to move around for the excitement of discovering new places to eat and shop and meet women. Sarah had pointed out that Debra was aiding and abetting what she herself called "foolishness beyond belief" and had received only a hurt sniff in response.

"Well, one thing's for sure. We can store our winter boots," Melissa said. "I was dreading getting mine out. It never rains in California."

"That's Southern California," Sarah said. "I asked a couple of people at work who lived in San Francisco. We can expect fog and cold rain for weeks on end. Apparently, however, just as we reach the edge of despair, the sun will come out and it'll be seventy degrees for a couple of days, then winter again."

"Sounds heavenly," Melissa said. "I hadn't realized how much I was dreading winter. I spent last winter in Minnesota and let me tell you, never again. Never again. I would walk around pinched and blue with scarves and vests and sweaters three inches thick while the natives would just be buttoning their top button."

Sarah laughed. "I've heard you have to live there a few years for the antifreeze supplements to work."

Melissa blinked at her, then smiled. "I can never tell when you're teasing me."

"That's not what you said last night."

Melissa giggled. "Are you going to stand there all day, or are you going to get something packed? I mean, if you're not going to be useful, the least you could do is come over here and kiss me."

Sarah shook her head. "The last kiss cost us most of the morning. We've got to be done by next Wednesday and you know it, missy."

"I can't believe that by next Sunday we'll be in San Francisco. I've always wanted to live there." Melissa looked up with what seemed like stars in her eyes.

Sarah looked across the valley at the mist-wreathed mountain. "I can't believe it either," Sarah said, not meaning to sound so wistful.

Melissa emptied her lap of photographs and joined Sarah at the window. "I know you'll be homesick, but I'll try to make it up to you." She feathered a kiss across Sarah's shoulder.

A flicker of pleasure warmed the suddenly cold pit of Sarah's stomach. Panic attacks, that's what they were, but they went away when she reminded herself of what she'd gained. She slipped her arm around Melissa and let the heat of her body chase away the rest of the fear.

* * * * *

"You really didn't have to come in today," Leslie heard Richard say.

A woman's low-toned voice answered him. "The apartment was such a mess that I just couldn't take it. And all my jeans were dirty, so here I am in the usual fright suit."

"It'll scare the programmers," Richard said.

My, my, Leslie thought, but he did sound friendly. If Sarah MacNeil was half as attractive as her voice, Leslie might begin to understand why he'd hired her without looking at another résumé. Meow, she thought. Richard's not that way.

She quickly yanked open her desk drawer and pulled out a small mirror. Her hair was presentable, but she wished she'd worn something other than an old T-shirt and black jeans. She'd forgotten that Sarah was starting today. And from the tone of Richard's voice, he'd clearly never discussed that Sarah officially worked for her. Nice way to start off, Leslie thought, feeling inferior and petty. Well, maybe it wouldn't be a big deal.

She shoved the mirror back in the drawer as Richard's voice drew closer. Sarah was laughing at something he'd said — for the third time in as many minutes. At least it was a pleasant-sounding laugh, not a donkey's bray or nerve-wracking titter.

"You there, Les? Ah, yes you are." Richard stepped back out of the doorway and gestured for his companion to proceed him. Lordy, lordy, he was being the perfect gentleman. "Sarah MacNeil, meet Leslie Stuart.

Whatever might have been her next thought was completely lost. She stared at Sarah MacNeil longer than she knew was polite, then somehow managed to tear her gaze away. Now she knew for sure that

Richard's gonads had played a part in his decision. She didn't know patent attorneys could look like cover girls — tall, slender, with a coil of light brown hair pulled into a casual ponytail. Melody had said the woman was some sort of athlete, but she was far from the muscle-bound troll Leslie had anticipated.

She simply had not expected someone so eye-catching. Get a grip, she shrieked at herself, completely unnerved. Richard was introducing Sarah and all Leslie could think about was blue eyes just turning to violet. If this was how *she* reacted, there were going to be testosterone problems in the programmers' cave.

"A pleasure," Leslie said, holding Sarah's firm, dry hand for a moment longer than necessary. She shot a glance at Richard. "Richard's told me a lot about you."

"I'm very glad to be here," Sarah said. "I hope you'll forgive the suit." She gestured down at the crisp navy blue linen. "All my casual stuff is dirty and we just didn't have the energy to do laundry yesterday. The apartment is a mess."

We? Leslie hoped Richard had heard that as well.

"I told Sarah she could have waited a day —"

"No, I needed to come in and get settled. It'll take far less time here than at home. My partner had some business appointments and I couldn't have faced any more unpacking by myself."

Leslie made herself think about dead kittens to keep from smiling. Richard's gonads had hired another lesbian — it was hilarious. She peeked at him. Well, if he'd understood the use of "my partner," the disappointment didn't show on his face.

"Well, when you're settled let me know, and we'll put our heads together," Leslie said. "Melody will show you more than you ever wanted to know about your phone and I think your computer is hooked up. If you have any problems with it we've got an entire room full of experts."

Sarah smiled. From the faint lines at the corners of her pale peach mouth, it was apparently something she did easily and often. "I'll see what I can do before unleashing the experts."

Leslie watched Richard escort her out of her office. He will still on his very best behavior and Leslie decided he'd missed the clues. Well, this would be interesting. And it served him right.

"Les, this can't be serious," Mark Davis said. He held out several pieces of papers. "Say it ain't so."

Leslie took the papers and glanced through them. She kept her annoyance out of her face as she scanned the memo from Sarah to all staff about security measures now in place. She hadn't read her copy yet, and she was still fuming that she hadn't seen it before it was released to everyone else. She knew Sarah had been hard at work on something — her printer had been clicking away for days. She just hadn't gotten up the nerve to go in and find out exactly what. What was she supposed to do, walk in and say, "By the way, in our extremely informal company you report to me, and I want to see everything you do before Richard does." She'd sound like a prima donna, and she cursed Richard for putting her in this awkward position.

The memo was damned heavy-handed. Instant termination for removing any copies of the program, any notes, memos or technical writing from the premises by any means manual, mechanical or electronic, or by any other means . . . blah, blah, blah.

"I work on it at home, sometimes," Mark said. "This is really inconvenient."

"Richard okayed it," Leslie said, "and it says Gene did too. We can't afford for anyone to lose a disk or have a friend of a friend poking around in someone's hard drive at home. You know this stuff goes on."

"No one even knows we're working on something," he said. "This is way overkill."

"As soon as we apply for the trademark name we'll have industry know-it-alls descending on us in droves. Besides, when was the last time you worked on it at home?"

"Okay, a couple of months ago. But I could have at any time," he said. "Other guys do. Miles proofs code during football games and Angie likes to do yoga in between runs."

"There's a TV here and we'll get Angie some mats, if that's what it takes. Look, I know this will take some getting used to, but you have to see it this way, Mark. It's in your best interests to protect the software from any prying eyes. You've got a couple hundred shares of stock by now that could increase ten or twenty times overnight. You'll be driving that Viper you've always wanted."

Mark grimaced, looking very much like Matt on meatloaf days. "Yeah, I guess. This is really a pain, though."

"Don't even think about testing the rules. It says there will be spot searches of backpacks and satchels and I'm sure Sarah means it. She hasn't said anything she didn't mean so far. And I would miss you."

"Pain in the ass," Mark muttered. Leslie frowned at him but didn't comment. Her own feelings were too close to his for her to chew him out. Mark suddenly shrugged. "But a nice pain in the ass, if you know what I mean." He wandered out of her office, leaving Leslie to wonder what everyone saw in Sarah — everyone but her.

"I have no idea why she doesn't like me," Sarah said. "But I can feel it. I'm glad I don't have to work closely with her. She said she wanted to review my action plan, but I really don't feel I should give it to her until Richard has approved it. She is, after all, just the marketing person."

Melissa helped herself to more rice. "Maybe she feels a little threatened. It's a small company and she's been queen bee for quite a while."

Sarah thought about that. She supposed it was just a simple case of jealousy, but Richard had such high esteem for Leslie that petty motives didn't seem in keeping with someone he'd respect so much. Of course she respected his opinion of people because he thought highly of her, and told her so, which meant her reasoning was getting rather circular. She shook her head to clear the confusion. "Could be. I get the feeling that I wasn't her choice for the job."

"Exactly what is her job?"

"Marketing and some administrative stuff, mostly. They use an outside accounting firm, but she's the liaison with them. They're talking about bringing in an accountant, though." Sarah looked up from the pad thai she was eating out of a container. Their neighborhood overflowed with good eateries and take out. "I'd welcome the extra dynamic in our little corporate structure. I'm not used to such a small company."

"But you like it, don't you?" Melissa looked up from the curried prawns in alarm.

"I like it very much," Sarah assured her. "Another bonus — there's an archery range about ten minutes from the office, so I can go practice for a break. Melody found it for me — I didn't even ask. She's a sweetheart."

"So is the woman administering my grant. She's been very helpful opening doors. There are art galleries in San Francisco around every corner. I think I want to do a whole segment on where you can find lesbian-created art in San Francisco and another on how lesbian-created art is displayed in non-lesbian settings, like the stuff they have at MOMA and the DeYoung."

"It sounds really interesting," Sarah said. "I'd love to see some of the exhibits sometime."

"I should have a script in another month, and by then I'll have met enough people to find the right women to do the production. Are you going to finish that?"

Sarah handed over the pad thai and half-listened as Melissa described several of the women she had in mind for her production. The other half her attention turned over the situation with Leslie. Leslie hadn't really done anything hostile. Just . . . well, it was the silence. Sarah had seen her with other people and knew she wasn't acting the same around her for some reason. Not as friendly, nor as forthcoming.

Give it time, Sarah thought. I don't need her eating out of my hand, but surely we can work together.

"So I think I'm going to try to do this as an ensemble. I read about it in the book by Kelli Martin. Did I tell you I met her?"

"No, I don't think so," Sarah answered. "Who is she?"

"I met her at a conference about a year ago. She

was promoting her book, *How to Produce Your Own Documentary*. It was great, especially since I never went to film school or really studied the process. She recommended a couple of ways to do it, and I'm going to try the ensemble approach. She said that if you have a compatible group of people, you can try to have a mutually supportive creative process. I can't think of anything more supportive than lesbians working on a lesbian project together."

Sarah opened her mouth to ask what Melissa *had* studied in school, then thought better of it. She was under the impression that Melissa had studied film, arts and theater extensively, which was why she wasn't following the more traditional route of learning by working on other people's projects. Instead, she said, "Well, sisterhood is powerful and all that, but I have heard some horror stories — basically that lesbians working together fall prey to the same problems as any other group. Shared lesbianism doesn't guarantee compatibility."

"I think I can avoid it if I follow Kelli Martin's method. We have to air a lot of issues and make sure that we really are compatible when it comes to politics, ethics, expressions of sexuality, animal rights, what art really is — really talk about things that matter. It takes longer, but the results can be really good. I talked to her about it when I met her. She was on a panel."

"If you think it will work, you should give it your best shot," Sarah said earnestly. She smiled. "I don't know anything about it at all, so you can ignore me completely. I'm just an English lit grad, with a minor in archery, and then there's that law degree — completely off your topic."

"English lit is perfectly respectable," Melissa said. "That law degree, though, well, I won't quote

Shakespeare —" She squealed when Sarah threw a pad thai peanut at her.

"Don't you dare," Sarah said. "Lawyering keeps us in pad thai."

"I know," Melissa said, sobering. "And I respect it."

"Thank you." She wondered if now was a good time to talk to Melissa about the money situation, which wasn't exactly great. Last month's hundred-dollar long-distance bill had been a shock.

"Let's go down to the Castro Theatre and see *Priscilla, Queen of the Desert*. It's only playing this week," Melissa said.

"I didn't see it the first time around," Sarah said, "though everyone said it was a hoot." She could hardly say money was a little tight and then agree to go to the movies, and she did want to see it. Give it time, she thought. Time will work with Leslie, and time will smooth this problem out, too, she told herself. They had plenty of time.

"They might not be willing to complain formally, but I've had a visit from four programmers in the last week over this."

Sarah paused in the outer office. She had a scheduled meeting with Richard, but apparently he was busy with Leslie.

"Les, you know they like to blow steam at you. Once they vent, you won't hear any more about it from them. Gene and I both thought these procedures were a good idea —"

"'Procedures' is a little mild, don't you think? They're CompuSoft all over. Instant termination is not something we do here."

"It is now," Richard said shortly.

Sarah realized they were arguing about the new security procedures. She knew she should quietly step out of earshot. Eavesdroppers never hear good of themselves, she heard Grannie MacNeil saying. But Leslie's next words kept her rooted to the spot.

"She's really won you over, hasn't she?"

"What's that supposed to mean?" Richard's voice was low and in a tone Sarah hadn't yet heard from him.

"When we discussed her résumé, I warned you I thought someone from CompuSoft would change MagicWorks into something we didn't like."

"If you think I hired Sarah because she's attractive I do believe I've never been so insulted."

"I didn't say that. Besides, in case you didn't figure it out already, she's gay. I was talking about CompuSoft's methods."

Aha, Sarah thought. Now I know where the CompuSoft fascist remark came from.

"Sure you were. Listen, Les, you and I both know it had to be done. And Sarah is willing to play the heavy and Gene and I were more than willing to be chicken and stand behind her. I don't know why you've got a bug under your collar about Sarah —"

"I do not!"

"You do so. And I knew she was gay."

There was a long silence and Sarah realized her face was hot with embarrassment.

"Well, aren't we the grownups," Leslie finally said. "I'm sorry, Richie. I guess I should have told you that I really resented your going over my objections the way you did. And ignoring the work I'd already done."

"Just because I'm a chicken shit doesn't make Sarah a Herbert."

Leslie laughed. "Not automatically. I just think she's proving herself to be one anyway."

What the hell was a Herbert?

"Look, we're still a warm and fuzzy place to work, but there's too much riding on what we do now for us to be sloppy. Sarah is disciplined, whereas you and I are not."

Oh, great. Leslie would really love being compared to her.

"Disciplined is one word for it," Leslie said in a scathing tone. "You and I used to make fun of people like her."

People like me? Sarah was so flummoxed she turned on her heel and quickly strode back to her office. She grabbed her competition bow and quiver from the corner, scrawled a note to Melody and slammed her way out of the warehouse door.

Fifteen minutes later she screeched into the parking lot of the nearby archery range. She'd been meaning to check it out for several weeks. She filled out the membership forms and plunked down a credit card. She was glad she hadn't made money an issue with Melissa, not when she was now indulging herself so thoroughly.

She strode to the far end of the range. It was fairly deserted and she didn't have to share the target. From 77 yards away, the gold center looked as big as her thumbnail. She nocked, sighted, focused and let fly.

Shhhhhhhwoshhhh-ipppp.

Bulls-eye. *So I'm disciplined, am I?* She nocked again and let fly. Bulls-eye. *A Herbert, whatever the hell that is.* She emptied her quiver of its twenty arrows in less than three minutes, shooting far faster than competition rules. She drew a long breath, released it slowly, then examined the target. A few

112

arrows were in the blue, and the rest clustered heavily in the gold and red.

"Nice shooting," a voice said from behind her. She turned to find an Asian man about her age stepping toward her. They shook hands and he said, "It's been a while since I've seen someone shoot like that. I guess I can assume you're *the* Sarah MacNeil."

Sarah arched her eyebrows.

"Tim Fukai I'm the owner, and when the clerk gave me your application I wondered if I could be so lucky, so I moseyed down to see."

"Oh, well, I guess I am *the* Sarah MacNeil. I never thought about it like that."

He looked at her bow with the curiosity all archers share, and Sarah handed it to him. "A little heavy, isn't it? What am I saying, obviously not for you. The full five feet, three inches?" He rested it on the floor and tapped the upper tip against his chin. "Hmmm. I have a feeling you don't need this," he said, gesturing at the stabilizer with its minimal weight.

"Looks funny without it," Sarah said. The bell rang, signaling a cessation of all shooting. Tim followed Sarah out to the target and helped pull the arrows free.

"Nice fletchings," he said, running his hand over the plastic feathers with their rainbow pattern.

"A gift," Sarah explained. Jane had given her the expensive Easton X10s with custom fletchings. In the final analysis, she valued them far less than the carbon fiber arrows she'd used in the Olympics, so she used the X10s for daily practice.

"Well, I'm glad you joined us," Tim said as he handed over the arrows he'd collected. "I don't suppose you have two hours a week to spare?"

"Not really —"

113

"For kids who need to develop a skill they can feel good about, as well as self-confidence. Kids who can't possibly afford to pay an instructor, and never one of your caliber."

"I've got a full-time job —"

"More than half of whom are girls who need positive role models if they're going to start thinking they're worth respect."

Sarah saw the fanatical light in Tim Fukai's eyes and had a feeling he wasn't going to take no for an answer. He began to smile as if he realized he'd gotten under Sarah's armor.

"I supply the range, bows and arrows, and you give them living proof that you can make something of yourself with practice, tenacity and just a little bit of skill. Put a little gold in their eyes, you know what I mean?"

Sarah found herself nodding. The man had the charisma of an evangelist. "I tell you what. You make it two hours on a weekday for eight weeks. Say four to six on Wednesdays — an after-school thing. I think I can talk my boss into that. And after that we'll talk again and see if we'll go forward."

Tim broke into an ear-to-ear grin. "I knew there was a reason to get up this morning. I love the sport, but I'm not a good teacher and I never made it past state championships. You're just what I've been looking for."

When she got back to work she met with Richard about her action plan draft and almost forgot that he and Leslie had been arguing about her. He enthusiastically endorsed her Wednesday afternoon schedule, being a big believer in anything that helped kids. But when she saw Leslie in the hallway she almost couldn't manage a smile. Richard was the one who really mattered. There was no reason she had to be chums with Leslie. So what if Leslie didn't like her. The feeling was mutual. But she was not going to let anyone make her feel inferior. It took two to tango and Leslie Stuart was not her idea of a dance partner.

"Now that you've have a month and a half to explore, how do you like our fair city?" Geoff nodded as the waiter proffered the wine bottle.

"I love it," Sarah said enthusiastically. "Really. I haven't been up to the Muir Redwoods yet, but I'll get there soon." She watched the waiter fill the glasses with a Napa Valley Merlot. "I hope I'm not going to end up with a thick head again. That bottle in Louisville knocked me out. And I love it here."

"It wasn't just the wine that knocked you out," he said. "Now that I have you all to myself, I want details, woman."

"Yeah, she knocked me out all right." Sarah shook her head in disbelief. "If your butthead of a co-worker had bet me I'd fall hard and fast for someone I'd just met and quit my job and leave Seattle in less than three months, I'd have wagered him everything I and my heirs will ever own in perpetuity, and been sure I was going to win."

"When do I get to meet this Circe?"

"Stop calling her that," Sarah said. "I have no desire to be cast as the drunken sailor. More wine, please."

Geoff laughed and topped off her glass. "You didn't answer my question."

"I would like you to come to dinner next week," Sarah said. "Melissa's a vegetarian, so I hope you like seafood."

115

"Love it. So how's your job turning out? Was I fool to pass up applying for it?"

Sarah made a yum-yum noise when the waiter delivered her Greek salad. She speared a calamata olive and savored its bitter bite before answering him. "Well, yes, you should have applied for it. With one exception, everyone is lovely to work with, the work is exactly what you would expect it to be, and there's a pleasant off-center quality to my boss. He looks like Santa Claus. Or Jerry Garcia."

"What's the exception?"

"Well, I've been there what, nearly two months now, and the marketing director still doesn't like me because I wasn't her first choice for the job."

"Sounds like a bitch," Geoff said. He fastidiously dabbed a crumble of feta cheese off his chin.

"It's not that she's nasty to me, and everyone else seems to worship the ground she walks on. She's kind of a mother figure, but I don't guess she's much past forty."

"You don't have to like everyone you work with."

"I know. She just raises my hackles. It's primal, I guess."

"Speaking of primal, our annual heterosexual strut is coming up and I wanted to make a date with you."

Sarah nearly choked on a piece of raddichio. "Heterosexual strut?"

"The company Christmas party. We always have them the weekend after Thanksgiving. I'd love to parade you around under their noses."

"Are you sure you want to do this, Geoff? It feels okay to you to give them what they want to see?"

"Not really," he said, chewing on his lower lip. "More and more I'm feeling hostile toward everyone I work with. I'd love to have them all hanging their

116

tongues out over you and then tell them you're a lesbian."

Sarah grunted. "Their tongues would probably still hang out. They have the thing that'll fix me, remember?"

"Well." He frowned into his wine. "Go with me anyway, just to see how the other ninety percent lives."

"Sure," Sarah said. "I'll wear something slinky. Melissa doesn't like dancing, so I'll really look forward to it."

"If I find a new job before then, I'll still take you out dancing."

Sarah grinned. "Good for you. You spend too much time at work to be miserable."

"Did anyone ever tell you that you have Robert Redford's eyes?" He raised his glass in a toast.

"Flattery is not going to get you anywhere," Sarah said. She clinked her glass to his.

"I know," he answered. "I love it." He leaned back to let the waiter set their entrees down. Sarah noticed the waiter was being especially attentive to them and the attraction was definitely not to her. Geoff glanced at Sarah's plate and said, "I thought you were a vegetarian."

Sarah already had a bite of filet mignon covered with crumbled Roquefort and a cabernet sauce halfway to her mouth. "Melissa's the vegetarian," she said, savoring the rich flavors. "It's the only thing we're not a hundred percent in synch over. And dancing, like I said. And the phone bill," she added.

"Oh, domestic bliss. Someday I hope for a little myself, but there are no princes on my horizon. So be happy if your honey makes lots of phone calls."

"I am. And I don't want to mention it to her. I don't want to get into anything remotely like because

117

I pay the bills she has to economize. That's not fair
to her. And it's not as if I can't manage it — I was
just surprised at the size of last month's bill. But I'm
sure it makes my socially responsible long-distance
provider happy."

"Trouble in paradise." Geoff offered her a bite of
his pork tenderloin with sliced portabellos.

The lemon-herb rub on the tenderloin made her
pucker a little. "That's delicious. I wasn't sure a
citrus flavor would work like that. Here." She
proffered a piece of filet liberally coated with
Roquefort and sauce. "No, it's not trouble in paradise, I was just surprised at the number and length
of the calls. But she's really working on her documentary and I suppose at some point the expenses
will be covered by the grant. I'm just not used to
having to watch my budget." Melissa's birthday was
December 23rd and Sarah was saving up as much as
possible for a laptop as a combination birthday and
Christmas present.

"I can feel my arteries hardening even as we
speak," Geoff said after he swallowed the filet.
"Money can bring down many a relationship. Don't
not talk about it because you have all of it and she
has none of it."

"It's not quite that bad. She sold her car to save
the cost of the unavoidable parking tickets — she got
nabbed by the street-sweeping patrol twice and that
was that. But the imbalance does make it hard for
me to bring it up. But I can live with phone calls,"
Sarah said. "We're hardly in the poor house. Hey, did
I tell you I'm teaching an archery class?"

"Not a peep."

"It's at a range not far from my office and the
kids are mostly great. It's only the second week, but
I think I'm going to like it."

"I didn't even know you played with bows and arrows," Geoff said.

Sarah sniffed. "I don't *play* with them. I went to two Olympics."

"Holy cow." Geoff paused with his fork halfway to his mouth. "Which ones?"

"Los Angeles and Seoul." Being with the kids had brought back all the good feelings about the competitions and the sheer love of the sport. She had told Tim Fukai that she was having so much fun she could almost be convinced she should pay him. She sipped her wine and then laughed at Geoff's still shocked expression.

"Wow," he finally said. "I'm so impressed. How on earth did you take up archery?"

She found herself telling him about Grannie MacNeil, about her stories of Welsh romance, and the farm in the Cascades that she had inherited, but hadn't seen in nearly two years. "It's really rustic, but I feel so rooted there. A neighbor keeps an eye on the cabin and even took care of a roof leak last winter."

"Sounds great. When I meet my Prince Charming I'll take him there and let the inevitable romance convince him to stay with me forever."

Sarah lifted her wine glass. "To incurable romantics."

Geoff clinked his glass to hers with a wistful smile.

6

*To love oneself is the beginning of a life-long
romance. (Oscar Wilde)*

"Go away, Gene, I've got a hangover," Leslie
heard Sarah say.

Oh, that accounted for the colorless face and
barely open eyes. Damn. She had found out yesterday
that Sarah's action plan draft had been on Richard's
desk for almost three weeks, and no one had seen fit
to tell her. She tried to be grown-up about it, and
she knew it was Richard's fault, not Sarah's. Well, if
she was being honest, it was her fault as well — she
just needed to talk to Sarah instead of hoping she'd
pick up on hints and suggestions.

She heard Gene laugh and Sarah's low-toned
rejoinder. Gene laughed again and Sarah said, more
loudly, "Have mercy, please."

Leslie returned her attention to the latest report

from the bank. She really, really, really wanted to hire an accountant, but Richard had been gone the last week acquiring video and audio equipment for the full-scale test of Tigger 0.2. There was a muffled crash from the other side of the warehouse and she felt a moment of pity for Sarah's head. Demolishing the previous occupant's telemarketing setup to make way for their staging and camera facilities wasn't particularly quiet, especially when the programmers started yelling at the construction workers.

"Maybe you'll want to shoot the breeze," Gene said from the doorway. "Sarah's hung. First time I've seen her less than bright-eyed and bushy-tailed. She told me to go do something that is anatomically challenging."

"You deserved it, I'm sure," Leslie said.

Gene looked at her quizzically as he sat down in her guest chair. He spoke in a lower tone. "You know, that's the first time you've said something supportive about her. What's with you two?"

"I don't know what you're talking about." Leslie knew she lied badly.

"I'm not the only one who's noticed. You're both nice people except around each other. Then you're both like magnetically polarized ice cubes."

"Ice cubes can't be magnetized," Leslie said.

"Oh yeah?" Gene's raised eyebrows reminded Leslie that he was the one with the advanced physics degree in addition to his other sheepskins. "Look, yesterday she asked me what a Herbert was. And you and Dick are the only ones who use the expression around here —"

"Oh shit," Leslie said, appalled. "She . . . must have overheard me and my big mouth shooting off like I was my kid or something. Damn. It's all my fault. Technically she works for me and I feel completely shut out of what she's working on, and I just haven't brought it up. I was hoping time would take care of it."

"Talk to her about it," Gene said. "She's not going to bite your head off. But not today," he added, hastily. "She's not really herself."

"Okay." Leslie pushed a stack of papers at him. "Be a darling and sort these for me. That is, if you don't have more pressing work to do."

"Bank statements? Ick."

"I'm done doing this all by myself — from now on all management gets to share the pain. I want an accountant in here."

"You have my vote," Gene said, holding the statements as if they'd been dipped in dog doo. "I guess I can sort —"

There was a burst of agitated voices from the direction of the Cave, then several doors slammed and more arguing ensued. Leslie could have sworn she heard Sarah moan. Gene quickly put the statements down without even bothering to hide his relief. "I think I'd better go see what that's all about. I'll come back."

"I believe that just like I believe everything Rush Limbaugh says."

"That is so cold, Leslie," Gene said as he disappeared.

Leslie sat back in her chair and doodled a pencil across one of the bank statements. So other people had noticed that she and Sarah weren't exactly friendly. It wasn't that surprising, and Leslie guessed she should do something.

She fished in her desk for a chamomile tea bag and a bottle of aspirin. She got a mug of hot water from the kitchen, dropped in the tea bag and then knocked quietly on Sarah's door jamb.

Sarah was munching slowly on a saltine and looked up from an unholy thick book. She hastily put down the cracker and sat up straighter, her eyes red-rimmed.

"Don't, don't," Leslie said. "Gene told me you were indisposed."

Sarah looked at the mug with a nervous swallow. "If that's hair of the dog that bit me, I might just be sick."

"It's tea. And here's aspirin."

"Ah," Sarah said. "The old remedies are still the best. I didn't have any tea at home." She reached for the mug and closed her eyes as she inhaled the light fragrance. "Thanks. I don't do this very often. For some reason when Geoff and I — he's a fellow patent attorney. When we get together we do destructive things with a couple of bottles of wine."

"Wine hangovers are the worst," Leslie said.

"Why is that?" Sarah took another sip of tea. "This is great."

"I don't know. I'll have to ask David — he's the one with the organic chem background. And he makes his own beer."

Sarah glanced up at her and there was an awkward pause.

"Listen," Leslie said, not quite knowing how to start. "Can we get together tomorrow, when you're feeling better? I think we have a lot of stuff to talk about."

"Let's talk now," Sarah said. "I'm not good for much else."

"You should go home. You look like death."

"Can't go home. There's a day-long meeting of minds going on in our apartment. My girlfriend is producing a documentary."

"How interesting," Leslie said. It figured that

someone as together as Sarah would have a girlfriend equally together. "Well, I guess we could talk now, if you're up to it."

Sarah nodded. "Look, I just want to get something off my chest before we talk about work. I know I wasn't your choice for this job, but I hope that I am proving to you that Richard made a good selection."

Leslie flushed. "That's kind of what I wanted to talk to you about. I saw the action plan you've developed and I was really impressed. But I also wanted to say that I need to be more included in your thought process, but I know that I'm partly to blame for the situation. Richard's to blame too, because I know for a fact that he never told you I'm technically your supervisor."

Sarah blinked. "No, he never told me that."

"He wouldn't. It's just the way he is. He's in charge of Gene and all the areas of programming and production, and I'm in charge of everything else. It used to be a really simple dividing line when we had two programmers doubling as tech support, and a couple of people stuffing MagicBullet into mailers and taking orders over the phone."

Sarah seemed to be choosing her words carefully. "It still . . . makes business sense. I just wish someone had told me. I can see how you must feel. I mean, in a company this size fussing about a chain of command can get out of hand. But you do need a little structure."

"And we have a little. Angie and Paolo work for me since they maintain the Web site and our on-line ordering system, along with their other work as Tigger programmers."

"Oh." Sarah slowly opened the aspirin bottle, extracted two, tossed them in her mouth and chased them with a swallow of tea. "It wouldn't have made any difference if Richard had told me. I'd have taken the job. He called you the marketing person."

Leslie sighed. "I'd slap him if we weren't best friends from way back. He's not being denigrating when he says that. He considers marketing, sales, negotiating and graphics to be great mysteries and he's in awe of anyone who can do them. So — infrequently, I'll admit — he's in awe of me. He is also in awe of accountants and lawyers." She nodded toward Sarah. "Oh, and plumbers."

Sarah smiled slightly. "I'm in awe of plumbers. Well, a lot seems clearer to me, so thanks for talking about it. I — I hope we can just start over."

"Not on the work you've done, which is great," Leslie said. "But on our working together."

"It's a deal. And thanks for the tea. I think I'll live."

"Hey, it's a mom thing. There's very little that hot tea and aspirin won't fix." Leslie hesitated for a moment, then decided to go for a complete truce. "By the way, you're not a Herbert."

Sarah opened her mouth, then snapped it shut. "How did — Gene can't keep a secret to save his life, can he?"

"That is a true statement," Leslie said. "What did he tell you it meant, anyway?"

"A fuddy-duddy." Sarah made a piffing sound into her tea.

Leslie chuckled and got to her feet. "He's mostly right. A Herbert is someone who is overly fond of rules and regulations and has no imagination. Like I said, you're not a Herbert."

"Thanks for the vote of confidence," Sarah said, with another wan smile.

Leslie felt better as she went back to her office.

So Sarah was a human being, not just an attractive suit with a black hole where the heart ought to be.

Sarah said a general hi to the half-dozen women lounging on various pieces of furniture and received a couple of "heya, Sarahs" in return. There were several new faces tonight. Melissa blew her a kiss.

She went to the bedroom, though she hardly needed to change out of jeans and a blouse, but if she lingered in the kitchen or living room she'd get pulled into the discussion. And after her significant *faux pas* last week, when she'd played devil's advocate on the question of capitalism versus socialism, she had no intention of getting caught up in another debate by the growing ensemble.

"I just don't think we should out anyone," Leeza was saying with her usual passion. "If the artist doesn't call it lesbian, then we shouldn't either."

"But then we're just going along with a lie." That was Janica, the pro-socialist debater from last week. "Someone has to name it so we can all own it."

Sarah closed the door and settled down in the rocker with the reading material she'd brought home, but she set it aside, feeling grumpy. She didn't want to stay cooped up in the bedroom. It was a beautiful fall evening, a little hazy, but the sunset was carnation pink and the temperature barely below 65. A drive up to Diamond Heights would probably yield a spectacular view, but the thought of shoe-horning the car back out of the garage, which she knew she was lucky to have — well, it was too daunting. A walk would be nice, she thought, and she could certainly use the exercise. She found an overshirt and headed for the door.

"Are you going out, darling?" Sarah turned to Melissa, who looked a little frazzled.

"It's really nice out," Sarah said, knowing she couldn't ask Melissa to go with her. They hadn't been out together in the evening for over a week.

"I don't suppose you'd bring back some eats? We're going to be at this for a couple more hours. It's getting pretty heavy."

Sarah's heart sank, but she managed a smile. "I'll pick up some vegetarian pizza."

"That would be great," Melissa said. "You're a doll."

The evening air was just edged with chill. Leaves crunched under her feet as she chose the uphill route toward Douglass. A Muni trolley rumbled by and after a few minutes of mindless plodding, to which she intoned, "You Can't Always Get What You Want," she stopped to look at the view.

The East Bay lights were just beginning to twinkle against a sky that had deepened to navy blue over the hills. A breeze had come up, and damp, cold air blew over her collar. She glanced up — yes, the fog was coming in. The gray waves fingered their way toward the Financial District, and Sarah knew they would soon blanket the city with a quiet akin to snow. She had come to love the air. It lacked the heady clarity of Seattle's, but it was rich with the sea and eucalyptus. She was beginning to sense the nuances of the different kinds of fog. This fog, brought in on the wind, would burn off slowly in the morning, promising sunshine for a few hours in the afternoon.

She caught herself sighing for what seemed like the hundredth time in the last week. She watched leaves curl and dance down the sidewalk and pondered her recent funk. Now that the situation with Leslie was smoothed out, she should be happy. Romance, Happiness and Fate were all satisfied. Her life should be perfect. Except it wasn't.

She hoped she wasn't just being jealous of Melissa's new friends and her documentary. Yes, it tied her up a lot of evenings, and they weren't making love at their pre-move rate, but that was to be expected. No one could keep up the pace they had set. If that was what was bothering her, she needed to get over it, and fast. Ellen would have called it poetic justice if Sarah couldn't handle a girlfriend with long work hours.

Okay, she told herself. Leave the negativity at the top of the hill. Tie it to an arrow and shoot it into the bay. She took a deep breath, then softly sang, "I've got sunshine, on a cloudy day," as she crossed over the two blocks to their favorite pizza parlor.

She felt braced and at peace until she went back to the apartment. Melissa beamed happily at her and invited everyone to dig in while Sarah went to the kitchen for plates and napkins. She noticed Janica helping herself to a large slice and thought cattily that she seemed to have no trouble enjoying the fruits of Sarah's capitalism.

She withdrew to the bedroom again with a slice of pizza and a glass of water, the liters of soda she'd bought a couple of days ago having been already consumed by the group. She looked disconsolately at the work she'd brought home, then, in a flash of inspiration, dug through her box of books in the corner. One of these days they'd buy some bookshelves to fit under the window.

Here it was, *Pride and Prejudice*, the copy she'd bought in Louisville and never opened. She settled down in the rocker to read.

Mr. D'Arcy had just insulted Miss Elizabeth Bennett's looks and disposition when the bedroom door opened.

"Hey, sweetheart," Melissa said. "You're still up."

Sarah saw with a shock that it was pushing ten o'clock. "I was reading an old favorite," she said. She held out the book and got up to stretch when Melissa took it.

"I could never get into Jane Austen," Melissa said. "Too dry for me."

"I've always found her hilarious," Sarah said. "I got into her after listening to *Northanger Abbey* on tape. Maybe that's the secret."

"Maybe," Melissa said, handing the book back.

"Mel, are you coming or not?" Janica's voice grated on Sarah's nerves, but she hid her irritation as she raised her eyebrows at Melissa.

"We're going to catch the last showing of *The Killing of Sister George* at the Castro. Want to come?"

It was the first time Melissa had invited her to join in the group for one of their social outings. Even though it would make her droopy in the morning, Sarah leaped at the chance. She bundled into her overcoat and clattered after the others down the stairs. It felt good to hold Melissa's hand as they walked down the steep incline toward the theater.

Leeza and Janica bickered all the way to the theater, and Sarah said *sotto voce* to Melissa, "Are they having some sort of love-hate thing?"

Melissa giggled in response. "I think so. Janica's practicing celibacy, but I don't think she's going to last much longer. Leeza's pretty persistent. Want a cookie?"

"You betcha, double chocolate chunk. I'll get the

tickets and meet you at the door." Sarah waited through the short line and handed Melissa her ticket in exchange for the cookie and, after an awkward head-tilt misunderstanding, a brief kiss.

"Come on, guys," Janica said. "We'll miss the beginning."

Melissa hurried into the theater as Sarah glanced at Janica. She wasn't prepared for the unveiled distaste on Janica's face. Sarah's hackles rose.

"After you," she said politely. Janica didn't answer as she stalked ahead of Sarah.

Pardon me for living, Sarah thought as she settled into her seat beside Melissa. Luckily, she neither worked nor lived with Janica, so she didn't really care what her problem was. It would be different if it were Leslie acting this way.

Sarah had seen the movie long ago on video but had forgotten how outdated and vicious the stereotypes were. The central character, an older actress who played beloved Sister George in a soap opera, was painted as a brutal butch who at one point forces her lovely and fragile femme girlfriend to eat a cigar. The scene was presented as if all lesbians behaved that way and Sarah joined the rest of the audience in hissing.

She had to control her laughter at the end of the film, however, because the theater had gone very quiet. She noticed a few other people holding back snickers, but they were far in the minority. She knew that the killing of Sister George in the soap opera was a metaphor, but she found the decision to film the death scene drunk as a skunk funny, heartening even. The character knew that she'd never be on screen again — her agent had found her a part mooing in a children's show. The movie closed with the young lover leaving her for a female network executive and the former Sister George sitting on the stairs, mooing with an edge of hysteria, but mooing nonetheless. Sarah wanted to applaud her will to survive.

After the movie, the three new faces, whose names she'd never caught, drifted toward the Muni stop, while the rest of them went in search of lattés and cappuccinos. Sarah was longing to head for home as well, but Janica, Leeza, Molly, Melissa and she crowded around a little table with barely enough room for their cups. Sarah stifled a yawn.

"Well, that was the biggest load of homophobic crap I've ever seen," Leeza said.

Molly, who spoke quietly if she spoke at all, said, "I rather liked it."

"Me, too," Sarah said. "Yes, it was homophobic, but given the odds stacked against her, I liked Sister George's tenacity."

Melissa sipped the decaf double-mochaccino Sarah had bought for her and looked a question at Janica.

"I'm with Leeza. They made a lesbian seem dirty and cruel, and then they stuck in a slapstick ending," Janica said. "They would never have treated a straight woman that way."

"Certainly not," Sarah said, too tired to hide her sarcasm. "They didn't do that in *Whatever Happened to Baby Jane* or, what was the movie Joan Crawford made? *Trog.* Straight women were treated with great respect in both those movies."

"Those were horror films," Janica said dismissively.

"And this wasn't? This movie came out in the period that started with *Baby Jane*, when older women were figures of horror. I think *Sister George*

131

had the same agenda underneath the lurid evil butch story. Sister George was not just a lesbian in this movie —"

"*Just* a lesbian?" Janica made it sound as if Sarah had just insulted the entire lesbian nation.

"Well, I don't know about you," Sarah said carefully, "but being a lesbian is only one facet of me. And it was only one facet of Sister George."

"I think since she stalked around most of the film looking dirty and menacing, *lesbian* is the label we're supposed to stick with," Janica said.

"Exactly," Sarah answered promptly. "Let's forget about her being old, fat and unattractive. Let's not think about how just being a woman made her disposable to the men who ran the soap opera. Susannah York is young and beautiful, and the worst thing that happens to her is inflicted by the evil butch. But Sister George loses her career and her dignity. I guess you could argue that butches get treated worse than femmes, but age and appearance are the real messages. At least that's how I saw it."

"I tend to agree with you," Molly said quietly. "I hadn't seen it before. I was watching and thinking about how, if I'd seen it when it was first released in 'sixty-eight, it would have depressed me so much because I was gay. But I thought about what any older woman must have felt seeing it. Because it wasn't a horror film. They were supposed to sit and laugh at the story of an older woman being discarded by her lover and her career. It reminded me of that saying about it being hard to laugh at the sight of your own blood."

Sarah decided right then that she liked Molly.

"You're talking as if you liked her character." Leeza leaned toward Janica, giving every impression of being totally in tune with Janica's every word. "She wasn't a character, she was a caricature."

"We're not supposed to like her," Molly answered. "We're supposed to find her disgusting, but I didn't. She is what her society made her, and in spite of it, she was going to survive."

Janica gave Sarah an evil look, as if Sarah was responsible for Molly's having a mind of her own. "What did you think, Mel?"

"I guess if I were going to review this movie, I'd have to stick with the lesbian context. It overshadows everything else, especially in the context of gay cinema."

Sarah tried to appear nonchalant as she sipped her decaf latté. It was too bitter, but there was only real sugar on the table. She had never felt the six years difference in their ages more than she did at that moment. And she was realizing that no one in Melissa's group seemed to be over 30. She remembered a billboard she'd seen earlier that day with a grungy, 20-year-old Mick Jagger wannabe hawking Calvin Klein cologne. Her first reaction had been that the last thing she wanted to smell like was how the model looked. And then she had felt old. She was too young to feel old.

Janica shot Sarah a triumphant look, then licked the coffee off her stir stick. Sarah shared a "whatever" glance with Molly.

"So, tell me," Janica said to Sarah, "if you're not *just* a lesbian, what are you?"

Sarah arched an eyebrow and thought that she didn't care enough about Janica to waste an arrow on her. "I'm a thirty-something woman, an attorney, a nature lover . . ." She thought suddenly of her archery class and Bryant, September, Sue, Tina,

Carrie, Pam and Dorothy. And Geno, what a sweetheart he was. She was finding herself more comfortable with the kids than she had thought she would be. "A teacher," she added, "and an archer."

"So multi-talented," Janica said in a flat voice.

"And a great lover." Melissa took Sarah's hand. "Kind and generous —"

"Oh stop," Sarah said in a voice that meant Melissa should go on for days if she liked.

Molly put her mug down with an air of finality. "I've really got to get going. Mel, can I make a suggestion for our next meeting?"

"Sure," Melissa said.

"Can we start putting an action plan down on paper? I'd like to have an idea how long we'll be working on this, and when I'll be needed the most. So I can plan, you know?"

"Sure, sounds like a good idea," Melissa said.

"I mean, I got an offer to do the lighting for another local documentary and they're asking me to commit to dates already."

"That's great," Melissa said. "You're probably right. It's time to get down to business."

Sarah blinked away the fog of sleep and her brain caught up to the conversation. The group had been meeting for over a month and they hadn't put anything on paper yet? They didn't have a production schedule? She looked at Melissa and made a mental note to ask about the terms of the grant. There must be a deadline or time limit. But it's not your grant, Sarah thought. Don't be co-dependent.

But it worried her. As they walked home she wondered how to bring it up and couldn't find a graceful way. She turned up her collar and unintentionally let a cold draft of damp air down her back.

134

"Chilly, isn't it?" Melissa snaked her arm around Sarah's waist. "I bet I can warm you up."

"As absolutely heavenly as it sounds, all I can think about is sleep. I have to get up in about five hours —"

"I promise to put you right to sleep." She preceded Sarah up the stairs to their door and turned back with the key in the lock. She unbuttoned her coat and slowly pulled her shirt out of her slacks. Sarah paused on the steps and looked up. The porch light outlined Melissa's golden hair, but her face was in shadow.

Sarah wanted to say, "I don't know you and I feel like I should," but her mouth was too dry to speak and the sight of Melissa unbuttoning her blouse too absorbing. At least that hadn't changed, Sarah thought. I still want her.

Everything would be okay, she thought. What was a little lost sleep to make everything okay? She surrendered to Melissa's eager lips and reveled in the heat of her body against the cold sheets. And for a while, with the world quiet outside, everything was okay.

"Is this your son?" Sarah picked up the framed photograph on Leslie's desk. In it a boy hung upside down in some sort of amusement park ride.

"Pride of my life and bane of my existence," Leslie said. "He's going on thirteen."

Sarah made a groan of sympathy. "I remember thirteen. My mother and I did not get along at all." They still didn't.

"We get along really well," Leslie said. "As long

as he does what I tell him to do. I've raised him to think for himself —"

"And it's such a bitch when he does," Sarah finished.

Leslie laughed. "You said it." She took the frame and ran a finger over the boy's face before putting it back in its place. "I love him to pieces. By the way, Mark Davis gets the prize for naming Tigger for the market."

"Was there a contest?" Sarah was startled by the abrupt change in topic.

"Not exactly, but all the programmers had an idea. His was Motion, and I've decided I like it. We can do a lot with the name both audibly and visually. Motion, ocean, notion, commotion, love potion. We can have some real fun."

"It sounds great," Sarah said. "I'll do a run on the trademark indexes and see if anyone beat us to it."

"Terrif. You can mark something off on the action plan. Hey," Leslie went on, "I got this invite to a dinner reception sponsored by ..." She dug through her top drawer, "Here it is, sponsored by Nestle. This year they're honoring Digital Queers for their commitment to empowering the gay community through technology," she read. "The keynoter is Wendy Fujamora from Sun Micro, who I think is possibly the smartest woman in computers today. Do you want to go with me? It's up your way — at the Grand Regency."

"Sounds exciting. Corporate dollars usually buy great meals. When is it and what do I wear?"

"Three weeks from Thursday. Last year I went — they honored Glide Memorial — and people were pretty dressed up. Something in basic black, cocktail-length would do." Leslie snickered and Sarah realized her shock was showing. "I may dress like this every day," Leslie said, with a wave at her jeans and T-shirt, "but under this scruffy exterior beats the heart of a woman who owns purple high heels."

Sarah chuckled. "I'll confess to having a few such items in my closet." She studied the invitation. "Cocktails at six. So why don't I bring my duds here and that way we can be the first at the whores dee-ovaries and free booze."

Leslie laughed outright. "Whores dee-ovaries?"

"Hey, that's what it looks like on the page. The first time I ever said it, I shocked my mother, who promptly told me to never say it again —"

"And you've been saying it that way ever since."

Sarah was grinning as she stood up. "Some things never change. Maybe I can get my girlfriend to drive me to work so we don't have to take separate cars. Parking won't be easy."

"It's a deal," Leslie said. "And if dinner is so beautifully presented — you know the type — a single curl of endive showing off the miniature carrot and a delectable bay scallop in a dollop of ginger cream — well, I know where we can get a greasy burger afterwards."

"I thought you were a health food nut," Sarah said. She nodded at the poster on Leslie's wall promoting Whole Farms Whole Fruit — Natural, Organic and Wholesome.

Leslie smiled was tinged with wistfulness. "I decided life was too short for tofu and bulgar. Just ask Richard. I corrupted him on the topic of food."

"Don't let her get away with saying I'm the one who drug her out of the commune and into business. Who came up with the Healthy Submarine stores?"

Sarah looked over her shoulder at Richard. "The commune?"

"Hey," Leslie said to Richard. "We franchised two locations. And I was ahead of my time. There's a Subway practically on every corner now, they're just not organic."

Richard inclined his head. "You were right. But we didn't know what we were doing —"

"As usual —"

"And the good thing is, now we do."

Leslie looked a little skeptical. "Like not hiring an accountant until *after* I commit suicide?"

"Hey, who's committing suicide?" Gene peeked over Richard's shoulder.

"Well, now that we're all here, let's have a staff meeting," Leslie said. "Agenda Item One: my imminent demise."

Richard and Gene groaned, but Sarah said, "Hey, I like staff meetings."

"I'm not kidding," Leslie said, running her hands through her already wild, black curls. "We have to make up our minds about accounting staff. I've got a half dozen things on my desk because no one else wants them and they're all finance type stuff. Which I hate as much as you do. We've put this off far too long, and we're getting big again and paying too much for outsiders to do it."

"Okay, staff meeting," Gene said. "Or she'll put stuff on our desks while we're away." He mimicked Leslie's higher pitched voice. "'Gene, be a darling and find out if there's some software that'll help us decide whether we should lease or buy the building.'"

Richard burst out laughing. His deep tenor sounded funny in falsetto. "'Richard, sweetie pie, the bank has messed up three times according to the CPA. Be a dear and check into that socially responsible bank you heard about.'"

Leslie tried to frown. "This is serious. I don't want to do this stuff and you don't, so who will?"

There was silence, then Sarah said in a panic, "Don't look at me!"

"Let's hire a financial manager," Richard said.

"And a bookkeeper," Leslie added.

Gene chimed in, "So moved."

"Seconded," Richard said. "All in favor?"

"Aye," they said in unison. Gene gave Leslie a high five.

"Let's let Leslie do the hiring," Richard said.

"So moved," Gene said.

"Seconded, all in favor?"

"Hey, wait a minute —"

"Aye," Sarah, Richard and Gene said.

Leslie pursed her lips. "Be careful what you vote for," she said in sinister tones. "You may get it."

"I'll help you review résumés," Sarah said. "And let's tell Melody that if anyone faxes one in it comes to you." She glanced significantly at Richard. "And no one else."

"High five, sister-friend," Leslie said. She smacked her palm against Sarah's, her face alight with laughter. Sarah felt a wave of pleasure. At last she was on the receiving end of Leslie's good humor.

7

The moments of the past do not remain still;
they retain in our memory the motion which
drew them towards the future, towards a future
which has itself become the past . . .
(Marcel Proust)

Thanksgiving for two turned out to be a lot of fun. The apartment oven was "efficiency"-sized and would never have held a turkey. Instead, Sarah had seen an advertisement for "The Wine Train" leaving from Napa and making a three-hour roundtrip to St. Helena, during which there would be wine tasting from many of the famous California vineyards. The jaunt was fun and diverting, and replete with delicacies in keeping with Thanksgiving.

Sarah had even booked a room in a nearby bed and breakfast in Napa so they wouldn't have to drive after the train ride. They tumbled into their quaint four-poster bed with giddy giggles and slept late on Friday. On their way home, they stopped in Sausalito and window-shopped with steaming lattés to warm their hands, then they wended their way through misting fog to sample fresh lobster for lunch at a little café on the wharf.

"Four-day weekends are so delicious," Sarah said, after a lazy Saturday morning. She lifted her head from the pillow. "Right there, left a little, down, oh —" She squeezed her toes together as Melissa found the exact spot where her back itched. "That's delicious, too."

"I'm actually glad the group decided to take a little break," Melissa said. "Molly was pressuring me to start putting things down on paper, but I'm having some new thoughts that I haven't processed yet. I'm going to go talk to the foundation about them on Monday and see what they think."

Sarah seized the opening she'd been looking for over the last couple of weeks. "Do you have some sort of deadline?"

"Well, not really. They gave me a limited amount of money and I have to make it last as long as possible."

"They gave you all of it up front?" Sarah was startled at the idea.

"No, they reimburse as I spend. I've submitted some living expenses that I haven't actually spent — how's that —"

Sarah stretched her back. "Perfect."

"Anyway, I haven't spent some of the money they have given me for living expenses because you pay for almost everything. I can use the money to pay for things I didn't budget for properly. Like I think the camera crew is going to cost more than I thought. And there's a symposium for new documentary filmmakers in Los Angeles I want to go to week after next. And I thought someone would donate film and developing, but now I don't think so."

Sarah was glad her face was buried in the pillow. She knew the shock she felt must show. After a minute, she took herself firmly to task. You're as bad as Leslie, she told herself, putting off an unpleasant topic because you don't want to be thought petty. But she needed to talk to Melissa about money. She hadn't told her she'd taken a pay cut. It cost more to rent in the Castro than it did to buy in Seattle. She hadn't wanted Melissa to feel guilty. But Melissa obviously didn't realize that between the rent, both of them eating out all the time, her transit passes and Sarah's commute cost to work, not to mention the car insurance, the rent on the garage, utilities, the long distance bill and the increasingly frequent meals Sarah was buying for the group — all in all, ends were barely meeting. And that didn't include luxuries — archery range membership, movies, theater, cable. The list went on and on.

It was obvious that Melissa didn't expect to contribute any of her earnings — from any source — to the household budget. It also bothered her that Melissa had told the foundation she had expenses she didn't have. Technically, it was fraud, though Sarah knew that there was latitude in every contract.

Sarah wondered what she could have said or done differently. She was feeling more like a patron of the arts than a lover. How was she going to bring it up? She hated talking about money. She and Ellen had never had to talk about it — they both had good jobs. And she knew exactly how Melissa must feel — it was how she felt when Jane had wanted to pop off to Switzerland to ski and Sarah had had to accept the trip as a gift instead of paying her own way. She hadn't liked the feeling of being dependent and Melissa must not either.

"I didn't really understand the San Francisco landscape, you know," Melissa was saying. "It's a lot more complicated. There's less stratification, and I'm thinking that is part of the story."

Sarah made a noncommittal noise from the depths of the pillow. Was she being petty? Did it really matter as much as the heat from Melissa's hands over her back, the intimate tangle of their legs, the way Melissa was slipping her hand between her thighs?

Sarah sighed with a mixture of unease and passion, not really liking the combination. Melissa was stroking her more insistently and her breath was hot against Sarah's neck.

"I love the feel of you," Melissa whispered in her ear. "Especially when you're so ready."

"I'm always ready — for you." Sarah shuddered to her hands and knees.

Melissa's fingers were sure in their path, and Sarah arched her back with a gasp.

"Is this what you want?" Melissa trailed her tongue over Sarah's ribs and then blew gently.

Sarah's entire body goose-pimpled. "Yes," she said, pushing her hips back against Melissa. At the moment she wanted nothing more.

"Matt, this is Sarah MacNeil," Leslie said, aware that her son was kicking his suitcase and ignoring her.

"How do you do, Matt." She extended her hand and Matt finally shook it. "Where are you off to?"

"Visit my dad," Matt said. "He lives in Hartford."

143

"Excellent," Sarah said. "It's already winter there. You can snowboard."

Leslie thought Sarah was pretty quick on the uptake. Matt's inline skates were hanging out of his backpack. Snowboarding, skateboarding and mountain biking completed the average 12-year-old's X games.

"Yeah," Matt said, brightening a little. "Dad says we're going to go up to a ski resort one weekend, which'll be great because my step-mom can't cook."

"Matt," Leslie said in a warning tone, even though she knew he spoke the truth. "Your dad can't cook either, so be fair. And if you can't say something nice —"

"I know," he said. He went back to kicking his suitcase.

Sarah shifted the thick file she was holding to her other hip, and said, "When's your flight?"

"I dunno," Matt said.

Leslie held back a sigh. "A couple of hours," she said to Sarah. "I'll run him up to the terminal and be back afterwards."

"Well, since you have some time, Matt, come into my office and I'll tell you how to make lasagna so you get at least one decent meal."

Matt looked less than enthused, but apparently it beat spending a boring hour with his mom. Besides, Leslie knew he'd perk up when she wasn't around. The sulks were for her benefit because she hadn't let him bring his Nintendo. Allan didn't want his other sons to be exposed to it, and she wasn't about to upset his household, not when she half regretted getting Matt the set he had. Matt could live without Nintendo for a couple of weeks, but he didn't think so.

A few minutes later she heard Matt laughing and she blinked back tears. She was going to miss him terribly, but it was his long break for the holidays and Allan's turn to have him for Christmas. He wouldn't be back until just before New Year's, nearly four weeks.

Sarah was making him giggle about something, then all was quiet for a long while. Leslie tried to work, but she kept looking at the clock and thinking it was another ten minutes closer to the time he would leave. She waited as long as she could, then went to see what Matt was doing.

She found Matt in the middle of a huge mess — he'd emptied all of the boxes in Sarah's office and was making stacks of gigantic books. "Matt, what on earth have you done?"

"I'm alphabetizing," Matt said. "Sarah said she never got the chance to put them in order."

The books were apparently law books, and each was as thick as a large rump roast. "Oh," Leslie said. "Thanks for giving her a hand."

"No problem," he answered.

"He's doing a great job," Sarah said to Leslie.

"Mom, look at these pictures I found. Sarah said she hasn't had a chance to hang them yet. She knows how to shoot bows and arrows."

Leslie studied the two framed photographs. It took her only a moment to pick Sarah out of the trio of women in each photo. Each stood beside an unstrung bow cradled into the crook of their arm. Leslie knew that Sarah taught archery. "You're just babies," she said.

Sarah nodded. "Don't we look young and brash? This one — from Los Angeles . . ." she took the photo and dusted the faces with her finger. "We do look like babies. I really changed a lot in the next four years."

"You grew your hair out," Leslie said, looking at

the more recent photo. The light brown curls had given way to a sophisticated knot more like the one she wore now.

"I had to pull it back or it would blow in my face at exactly the wrong time. It's hard to aim at something with hair in your eyes."

"Cool," Matt said. Leslie hid a smile as he carefully brushed his hair out of his eyes. "I don't know anyone who can shoot a bow and arrow."

"I'd be happy to teach you sometime," Sarah said.

Matt jabbered questions at Sarah, as animated as Leslie had seen him in recent months. Sarah answered him patiently, shooting a conspiratorial glance at Leslie. Leslie smiled her thanks, then felt herself getting misty, so she ducked out with a mumbled explanation and headed for the ladies room.

She was blowing her nose when Sarah came in, a sympathetic look on her face. "How long is he going for?"

"Four weeks. It'll be our first Christmas apart in three years. His dad was really great about the last couple years, but he's getting old enough now — Matt, not Allan. I mean, Allan doesn't need him any less than I do just because he's got two more boys," Leslie said, knowing she was babbling. "It's not fair to Matt. He's really excited about going, but we had a fight this morning."

"He won't sulk about it for long, he doesn't seem like that kind of kid," Sarah said. She scooted up onto the counter and swung her jean-clad legs. "My parents got a divorce when I was eight. My mom had me for the school year in San Diego and my dad for the summers wherever he happened to be — and I stayed a lot at my Grannie's. I don't think I ever left my mom without having a fight beforehand. But I

146

was glad to see her when I went back. At least until I got older and fighting became our only way of communicating. I was not the daughter she ... expected."

"We don't fight much," Leslie said. "We squabble over little things, like lights out, and snacking between meals, that sort of thing." She flashed suddenly on what she would find when she got home — his cereal bowl waiting to be rinsed, the swags of red and green construction paper loops across the living room, and the tree they'd put up this past weekend for their own holiday celebration. "I'll be fine —" she said, and then to her mortification, she began to sob like a child.

Sarah slid off the counter and pulled Leslie into her arms, patted her back and whispered, "There, there, it'll be okay," as good as any mom. Leslie hadn't realized that Sarah was several inches taller, and she let herself relax for a minute, soaking up Sarah's sympathy, then she straightened up, aware that she was liking the warmth of Sarah's body a little too much.

"I told myself I wasn't going to cry this time until after he got on the plane. I'm always a mess when he goes away."

Melody came in, took one look at Leslie and said, "He'll come back." She glanced at Sarah. "I forgot this was the big day or I'd have brought some of my mom's chocolate toffee in."

Leslie blew her nose and splashed water on her face while Sarah and Melody discussed the merits of homemade toffee. "I look like hell," she said to her reflection. "He's going to know I was crying."

"He's going to know you're human," Melody said. "He's a lucky kid, and he knows that too."

147

From the doorway Sarah said, "I'll go find out what he's up to. He was eyeing my computer when I left, and I'll bet he's playing Free Cell."

Leslie nodded and took a deep breath. "I'm going to be okay," she said to Melody. "I usually only cry once, and I thought I'd make it until after he was gone."

"Well, look at it this way," Melody said slyly. "This time it was Sarah's shoulder you got to cry on."

"What's that supposed to mean!" Leslie rounded on Melody in indignation.

"I just meant that her gay little shoulders probably felt better than my straight ones." Melody was looking far too innocent.

"There's nothing wrong with your shoulders," Leslie muttered. "And Sarah's are a little pointy, if you must know." She tossed her tissue into the trash and headed for the door.

"Um-hmmm," Melody said. "Methinks —" Leslie closed the door before Melody got as far as "doth protest."

Matt's sulks were a thing of the past when Leslie finally went to collect him from Sarah's custody. She didn't look too weepy, she hoped, and Matt, proud of the neatly arranged books he'd put on Sarah's shelves, didn't notice anything amiss.

Or at least she thought so, but as they pulled into the airport parking garage, he said, "I wish you could come with me."

"I know, honey. And I wish I could too. But it's not the way things are."

"I know." He helped pull his suitcase out of the trunk and set it on its wheels. "But you gotta promise you won't sit around and eat chocolate while I'm gone. It's not good for you."

His tone was such a close match to her own when she nagged him that Leslie almost laughed, but she knew he was sincere. She followed him through the parking lot saying, "I promise. I'll go to the movies. I'll buy myself some new jeans. Hey, I'm going to a fancy dinner on Thursday night with Sarah."

"You are?" Matt pulled the suitcase onto the elevator. He was looking speculative.

"Sarah has a girlfriend," Leslie told him. "It's just a business dinner."

"Oh."

"But I'm sure I'll have a lot of fun. And I'll turn the temperature on the hot tub up to where I like it."

Matt wrinkled his nose. "Just remember to turn it down before I get home."

"I will." She was proud of herself when she didn't cry, not even when Matt gave her one of his rare kisses. She waited until his plane taxied away from the jetway. Back in the car, she sniffled in privacy and did not think about Sarah's shoulders, nor the empty house that would greet her.

"So how did your meeting with the foundation go?" Sarah bit into the spring roll she'd liberally spread with hot mustard.

"Not very well," Melissa said, not unexpectedly. Sarah had known something was wrong from the moment she got home.

The hot mustard made her eyes water. She blinked furiously. "Wow, that sure does clear the sinuses."

Melissa smiled, though it didn't reach her eyes.

"They weren't very supportive of my new idea even though I think it'll be a better documentary if I change things." She pushed the chow mein around on her plate. "I didn't realize how integrated San Francisco is."

"Integrated? You mean racially?"

"No, men and women," she said as if stating the obvious. "The lesbian and gay communities are really woven together. A lot of the lesbian projects are given venues by gay men."

"Well, isn't that just an example of *noblesse oblige* on the part of the men?"

Melissa shook her head. "I don't think so. Because the artists are pleased with the display space, and the men seem to want to keep everything the way the artist intended. They're not imposing their ideas on the artist, but instead giving them exactly the space they need."

"Oh," Sarah said, feeling completely at a loss.

"And a lot of the gay art projects are done collaboratively by men and women. If I want to talk about the women's projects I have to include the men because it's relevant. The grant money was raised specifically to highlight lesbian projects, so the foundation doesn't want projects co-produced with men in the documentary."

"Well, it is what you originally proposed, isn't it?"

"Yes, but now I know better. I can even get free studio time from the public TV station, which will save oodles of money, so I'll have more for other things. Like Janica has spent a lot of time on interviews and wants to do a preliminary videotape, and of course she expects to be paid something for her work, which is only fair. So if I got the free studio time I could pay her, and it's a gay man that's offering it. Everywhere else I've lived the men have been real condescending and standoffish. But it's different here."

"But what about —" Sarah realized she was on the verge of sticking up for Janica.

"What about what?"

"Well, isn't one of Janica's points that it's really hard to do anything without the men getting involved? That sometimes they're helpful to the point of smothering? And other times won't lift a finger to help a lesbian project?" Melissa had been the one to stop working on a book because her collaborator had borrowed money from a man to finish it. Sarah caught back the words because she didn't want to . . . start something that might not end well.

"I guess that's true. Janica isn't going to be thrilled about the change in plans, but she knows we're doing something important."

"But I thought you said the foundation didn't go along."

"They didn't, but I think I can talk around them. Or I'll apply elsewhere for a different grant and give theirs back." She shrugged and took her plate to the sink.

Sarah blinked dumbly at her sweet and sour shrimp.

"Are you going to finish that? I skipped lunch." Melissa reached for the container.

"All yours," Sarah managed to say from her suddenly tight throat. "There's a couple of pieces of shrimp at the bottom." She studied Melissa's fingers as they gripped the chopsticks. She was feeling disembodied, almost numb, and she didn't know why.

* * * * *

151

Leslie heard catcalls and whistles and gave up her last pretense at working. She didn't want to name the emotion she was feeling, but every time she thought about the evening she was about to spend with Sarah, she got butterflies, like some idiotic teenager. She'd best go find out what the fuss was all about to get Sarah out of her head.

When she saw the reason, she found it difficult to swallow. Sarah had changed for dinner and she hadn't been kidding about the black cocktail dress. The sequins glittered even under fluorescent lights, and the simple lines of the dress suited Sarah's figure perfectly.

"Down, you animals," Sarah was saying. "You'd think you'd never seen a dress before."

Mark said, "You clean up real good," while Angie and Melody evaluated the fabric as if they were considering buying it.

"This is just a jacket," Melody said. She lifted the lower corner to reveal a great deal more of Sarah's thigh before a tight black skirt came into view.

"Yeah, but I usually don't take it off." Sarah shook the jacket out of Melody's fingers and smoothed it over her hips again. "The dress is a little too revealing for my quaint old heart."

There was general encouragement for Sarah to take the jacket off, which Gene ended with, "Knock it off, youse guys. Sarah's not a pin-up."

Greg, whom Leslie had never heard utter more than two words at once said, "Sometimes the Nineties suck."

Sarah laughed and Leslie realized she'd gotten used to the frequency and tone of Sarah's laughter. "Sorry it's not the Sixties, Greg."

"Yeah, I suppose. If it was the Sixties, you'd be a

guy." Greg looked sidelong at Mark. "Mark might like that, but I prefer you the way you are."

"Hey," Mark said indignantly. "I like Sarah the way she is too. And unlike some people, I *have* a relationship."

"Truce," Sarah said with a puppy-shooing gesture. "Thank you all for your compliments. I think it's time for me to exit stage right."

Leslie held the door open and gave Melody a look that said, "Don't you dare say that Leslie prefers Sarah the way she is too. Don't you dare."

Melody's smirk said she had considered it, and deserved brownie points for keeping her mouth shut.

"I'll go get changed," Leslie said to Sarah as the door to the Cave closed. "They've seen me in a dress, so there won't be another riot."

"I bet you clean up real good, too." Sarah's office phone rang and she ran to catch it. Leslie couldn't believe anyone could move that fast in heels. Sarah would ruin any of Matt's favorite horror movies — the monsters would never catch her, heels or not.

Sarah had been right about the parking situation. They ended up paying a valet to stow Leslie's Volvo in the hotel garage. They wasted no time in scavenging the best "whores dee-ovaries" and took turns standing in line at the bar. When the dining room opened, Leslie was already feeling the better for the mellow Cabernet she was sipping.

They shared their table with four other same-company couples, all infected with the networking bug. Leslie found herself talking nonstop to the two people who worked for Silicon Graphics while Sarah chatted with someone who had also once worked for CompuSoft. There was a free-for-all business card swap and before Leslie knew it, dinner was over.

Then the lights went down and the dinner sponsors began the long parade of thanks to the hard-working volunteers at Digital Queers. The ceremonies took less time than Leslie had expected, then there was a surprise bonus — a DJ and dancing.

A male/male couple at their table immediately headed for the dance floor, closely followed by the man and woman from the investment company. One man, who had been talking mostly to Sarah throughout dinner, addressed the entire table. "Somebody dance with me. It's hard being single."

Before anyone else could say yes, Sarah was on her feet and shrugging out of her jacket. "I was hoping someone would ask," she said.

Leslie was glad Sarah hurried to the dance floor with him. She was finding it difficult to swallow. It wasn't often that she was speechless and she was afraid if she opened her mouth all that would come out was a wolf whistle worthy of a construction worker. Under the jacket Sarah wore a strapless thigh-high sheath. Her body wasn't perfect, which made it all the more alluring. Her belly swelled like a woman's, not a boy's, and she did not have buns of steel. And the cleavage — well, that's what took Leslie's breath away. Lightly muscled arms, straight spine, firm calves — she shuddered in places that hadn't shuddered in quite a long time.

She was going to have dreams about slowly lowering the zipper of that dress, taking Sarah's breasts in her mouth, exploring the contours of Sarah's body. What would it be like to dance with her, to hold that body against her own? Why hadn't she realized that the personality she had come to admire was accompanied by a body she'd die for?

This sucks, she thought. Sarah works for me. But

that zipper would come down so easily ... "I'm sorry, what did you say?"

A tall woman in a pinstriped suit had paused next to her chair. "Would you like to dance?"

"I'd love to," Leslie said. She'd lost Sarah in the crowd, which was just as well.

Her companion turned out to be a more than passable dancer, and when the music segued to a two-stop, they stayed on the floor. Just then, Leslie made eye contact with Sarah and she smiled gaily as she and her partner joined the swirl of dancers. When she glanced in Sarah's direction again, Sarah was still looking at her, and with the oddest expression on her face.

Though they danced well together, Leslie had to take a break. Sarah was just coming on to the floor again, this time with a woman who swung her expertly into the salsa beat. After that, Leslie lost track of Sarah's dance partners and barely kept track of her own. All she could think about was not thinking about Sarah. The harder she didn't think about Sarah, the more she thought about her. It was really not a good thing, and yet she couldn't stop herself.

It was almost midnight when Sarah finally collapsed into her chair. Leslie had only been seated a few moments herself.

"I'm bushed," Sarah said. "I had no idea there'd be dancing. This was great. I'm going dancing on Saturday night, too, so my cup runneth over. Thanks for asking me."

"My pleasure," Leslie said. "Did you take dance lessons?"

"Well, let's just say I've had private instruction," Sarah said with a laugh. Her cheeks were flushed and her eyes were mostly violet. "You know, I have to ask you something, and I hope you won't think I'm being nosy."

"Ask away."

"Are you a lesbian?"

"Oh!" Leslie felt herself blush. "I — yes. I just realized we've never really acknowledged that we have that in common."

"My fault," Sarah said. "I think I would have assumed it except for Matt. Which was quite unenlightened of me."

"Yeah, there's Matt to explain."

"You don't have to explain to me," Sarah said. "Really, it's none of my business."

"Well, someday I will. For now, let's just say I went through a phase and Matt was the result."

Sarah chuckled and then leaned over to pick up her jacket, which had ended up on the floor. Leslie told herself to ignore Sarah's cleavage then thought if she looked away everyone would know she'd been looking, so she kept looking, then had to drag her gaze to the centerpiece when Sarah straightened up.

Sarah fanned herself with her dinner napkin. "Shall we go? I can't wait to cool off outside."

Sarah preceded Leslie out to the curb. Leslie handed over the parking stub and they waited under the hotel canopy for the car. The night was clear and cold and Sarah inhaled deeply.

"The air is great here. Almost as good as Seattle."

Leslie realized that Sarah had a mark or smear of some sort on her shoulder blade. "Wait, you've got something on your back," she said.

"What?" Her back muscles rippled. "Please don't tell me it's a bug."

"I don't know what ... Oh! It's a tattoo. I'm sorry."

"Oh!" Sarah glanced over her shoulder, her nose wrinkling. "I know it's small, but it's not a bug."

"What is it?" Leslie peered at it, then recognized the symbols. "Why do you have Olympic rings on your back?"

"Tradition," Sarah said. "The men back out all the time, but we women believe in tradition."

"No shit," Leslie said, feeling her jaw drop. "You went to the Olympics?"

Sarah turned all the way around with a grin. "You really didn't read my résumé, did you? It's right there."

"I am so impressed. I've never known an Olympian before."

"Well," Sarah said, turning back to the car, "you might think that. But we're everywhere. Aren't you glad you haven't been telling Olympic jokes around me?"

Speechless for the second time that evening, Leslie could only think that Sarah was one surprise after another. She'd expected a one-dimensional attorney but Sarah had dimensions Leslie didn't even know existed.

"My girlfriend is probably still up, if you want some coffee," Sarah said as they pulled up in front of the apartment building.

"No, I'm fine. I stopped drinking about two dancing hours ago." Leslie hadn't actually met Sarah's girlfriend, but she'd seen her once when she had picked Sarah up after work. She felt a little thud in the region of her stomach and realized she had needed a reminder that Sarah wasn't in the market for a new girlfriend, just as she herself had told Matt only two days ago.

"Well, see you tomorrow," Sarah said as she got out of the car. "I had a lot of fun," she added.

If only, Leslie thought as she drove home. If only Sarah had put her jacket back on, then Leslie might not have spent the next several hours trying to get the image of Sarah's thighs out of her head. If only almost-forty women with offspring didn't produce anti-endorphins in every eligible lesbian they met. If only Xena Warrior Princess would backflip into her bedroom.

Sarah

ROMANCE (ro-măns, ro"măns')
[Middle English, from Old French *romans,*
romance, a work written in French from
Vulgar Latin] romance (noun); romanced,
romancing, romances (verb)
1. A strong, sometimes short-lived attachment,
   fascination, or enthusiasm for something
   or someone.
2. Ardent emotional attachment or involvement
   between two people, characterized by a
   high level of sincerity and devotion; love.

8

. . Motion is a harmony, and dance
Magnificent.
(William Wordsworth)

"I hope that I get a chance to talk to people about what I'm going through with the foundation," Melissa said. She snapped her suitcase shut and turned to Sarah. "You don't mind my being gone for four days, do you?" She ran her hands under the waistband of Sarah's sweats.

"Really, I don't, enjoy yourself. I'm sure the symposium will be very helpful. Besides, I'm going to that Christmas party tonight, remember?"

"That's right," Melissa said with a pout. "Having fun with some guy."

"Who likes to dance, and you don't," Sarah reminded her. She rubbed her nose against Melissa's.

161

Melissa kissed her, then sighed. "I guess we'd better get going or I'll miss my flight."

Sarah was unsettled by the knowledge that she was rather glad Melissa would be gone for a few days. She needed some quiet and the last week — certainly brightened by the evening of fun she'd had with Leslie — had nevertheless been stressful at home. Melissa's unhappiness pervaded everything she did. They'd be talking about something else and Melissa would refer to "it" and Sarah would always know that Melissa was referring to the "situation" with the foundation.

She needed to think. She could hardly tell Melissa she thought the foundation was in the right. After all it was their money given on specified terms, and Melissa was not making a minor change to her proposed project. Why did she have to listen with a critical ear, not a supportive one? Melissa had never asked for Sarah's opinion, only her support. What did it matter to Sarah if Melissa ended up turning down the grant? She didn't know the answer — but she knew it mattered — it mattered a lot.

On the drive back from the airport she went on cross-examining herself — the more Melissa complained of feeling trapped and ill-used, the less sympathetic Sarah felt. She wanted to tell Melissa about law school, where unfairness was so monumental it drove some students to suicide. And was it fair when you lost a match because a tiny puff of wind put your arrow a hair's breadth out of the gold — or won because the puff caught someone else's arrow?

Life was not fair, she wanted to tell her, but Melissa had dreams, and she didn't want to quash them. If she'd learned anything in life, though, she'd learned that dreams didn't come true by wishing — it took hard work, perseverance, focus.

Where was the passion she had felt only a few weeks ago? Where was Happiness? Where was Romance?

Had it gotten muddied by the money? How shallow that would be, Sarah thought. How stupid to jeopardize the feelings she had for Melissa because of a few dollars.

She sat in the living room and looked out at the city she was coming to love. She wouldn't be here, wouldn't be changed for the better, if not for Melissa. Living here had let her discover a love of teaching and a genuine affection for kids — she looked forward to her classes more than she had thought possible. She felt more a part of developing a software product than a cog in a machine protecting one. She liked the everpresent babble of the programmers instead of the speakerphone conversations of other attorneys. Seattle still called to her, but she had Grannie MacNeil's farm — her roots were safe.

She owed this new sense of self to Melissa, or to her love for Melissa. A love she'd never declared, she reminded herself. They'd never talked about forever, or commitment, or monogamy for that matter.

She had never told Melissa about the Olympics, never really given her anything of herself except her body . . . and her checkbook. Could she blame Melissa for not giving back more?

She continued to brood as she dressed for Geoff's Christmas party. She started to put on the same dress she'd worn with Leslie, having picked it up from the dry cleaners the day before, then something made her put it back in the closet. She did want to make an impression on Geoff's co-workers, for Geoff's sake, but not . . . well, she had really worn the dress for Leslie, to dismiss any last vestiges of Herbertness from Leslie's image of her.

She selected instead a dress better suited for dancing, in deep emerald with a sequined bodice. It was a gift from Jenny, the ballroom dancer, and had a flaring skirt, high-necked halter, and a dramatic plunge to the small of her back — at least it appeared backless. There was actually a closely matched flesh tone fabric of Spandex and cotton blend that allowed a wide range of movement, covered her bra straps and kept rivulets of perspiration from running down her back. Black seamed hose with flocked roses at the ankles made her feel decidedly rakish, and she hoped Geoff appreciated the time it took to get them on properly.

She was waiting at the window when Geoff's taxi pulled up and she hurried out the door to save him the walk up the stairs. He whistled when he saw her, which reminded her of the programmers at work, and she twirled as she reached the street.

"You look great in a tux," she told him. "Will I do?"

"You'll do, sweet thing," Geoff responded. "I will be the envy of every man there."

"I don't know about that," Sarah said, settling in the taxi. "But I'll ruffle your tie and gaze adoringly into your eyes, because I said I would . . ." She hesitated, because she didn't want to seem judgmental and ruin their evening.

"But you don't really accept that it's necessary. Well, neither do I," Geoff said. "I'm a finalist for a job at Carsey-Mellon Foods —"

"Wow," Sarah said. "That's a huge outfit. I bet their legal department is up there with CompuSoft's in size."

164

"I think so. And they have a gay and lesbian employee group *and* domestic partners benefits, not that I have one of those. I'd sacrifice the last ten percent of my pension vesting if I left H and G, but I'd be a lot happier. I hate biting my tongue when they make remarks about Hawaiian marriages, and last week someone was reading a snip from the paper about the increasingly lower turnouts for the annual memorial march for Harvey Milk and said it was good riddance. I wanted to punch him. I'm afraid I will one of these days."

"Let's dance the evening away," Sarah said soothingly. "Just don't get me drunk like last time — I had a hangover that nearly killed me."

Geoff chortled. "I didn't have any ill effects, but then you finished that last bottle all by yourself."

"Did I? No wonder. You're a bad influence."

"Hah!" He promptly insulted her morals and they bickered the rest of the way to Kyoki's. Geoff kept his hand proprietorially in the small of her back as he shepherded her through the lobby to the large banquet room. She didn't remind Mr. Butthead, when Geoff introduced her, that she had seen him before at a hotel in Louisville. They sampled sushi from the buffet, then tossed off a thimbleful of warmed saki that burned deliciously all the way down. Most of the banquet room was devoted to the dance floor, and a four-piece ensemble was tuning up.

"That's Mr. Hansen, the H of H and G Chemical. And his wife, Lorraine," Geoff whispered in her ear. "G is no longer with us, and all of the corporate culture springs from Mr. Hansen's narrow brow."

His brow looked plenty narrow, Sarah thought. He was roly-poly in a Burl Ives sort of way, but his expression held such superiority and disdain that she instantly disliked him. "How do you get along with him?" She could tell that most of his staff was afraid of him by the formal way they approached him, the physical distance they kept while they talked and the hint of bowing in their demeanor as they left.

"I don't. I talk to my boss, and he talks to Mr. Hansen. I'm considered a very junior member of the firm."

"After what, seven years?"

Geoff nodded. "I'm sure it's because I'm not married, and therefore not a settled, mature sort of fellow, the kind they like to see in their upper management slots."

"Like something out of the Fifties."

The music started with a swing version of "Jingle Bells." No one danced, though Sarah could tell that many, like her, were itching to.

"What's the deal?"

"I told you it was a heterosexual strut. They practically reenact their effing weddings. Here it comes," Geoff said. "Mr. Hansen will dance with Mrs. Hansen. After two minutes, Mr. Wells, *senior* executive vice president, will cut in, and then Mr. Hansen will ask Mrs. Wells to dance."

"When it would be far more amusing if he asked Mr. Wells dance," Sarah added, her tone dry.

Geoff nearly choked on his California Roll, drawing a few disapproving glances from several people. Sarah was certain that her remark had been overheard by the younger couple near them — the woman was covering her mouth with her napkin, while the man turned his laugh into a cough. The woman strolled over and extended her hand.

"Teresa Griffith," she said. "Are you here with this bad boy?"

"Sarah MacNeil," Sarah answered in kind. They

shook hands politely, then Teresa introduced her husband, Carl.

"Teresa is a product manager I work with," Geoff explained. "And she has no right to call me a bad boy."

"Geoff, darling, I've had a little too much saki way too quickly and the night is young," Teresa said. "So you'll have to excuse my manners. But take a look around you sometime. I know, we all know —" She abruptly stopped and shot a panicked look at Sarah.

Geoff flushed. "When you do my performance evaluations we'll talk."

Carl put his arm around her shoulder. "Honey, you *have* had too much saki." He gave his wife a meaningful glance and then flicked his gaze at Sarah.

Teresa blinked at him, then smiled. "Quite right, darling. I'll be good."

"It's all right, Teresa," Sarah said. "Geoff and I are just friends. I like him just the way he is."

"Thanks for the vote of confidence," Geoff said. "Can we stop talking about me like I'm not here?"

Teresa leaned toward Geoff and spoke in a lower tone. "My brother wasn't asked and didn't tell and he still got discharged."

Sarah could tell that Geoff was uncomfortable. His color was high and he looked as if his collar was two sizes too tight.

"Terry, leave the poor man alone," Carl said.

"Sorry, Geoffrey, my love," Teresa said. "I'm a mom and you've still got your boyish good looks, so I can't help but nag you."

"No problem, Big T." Geoff cleared his throat. "Thanks for your support. Know what? I think we can all dance now."

Something devilish seized Sarah, and she said to Teresa, "Would you like to dance?"

Teresa gaped. Carl spluttered into his wine and Geoff burst out laughing.

"I don't wait to be asked," Sarah said as Teresa laughed until she got tears in her eyes. "I just tell."

"That served me right," Teresa said. "I'm not going to assume nothing about nobody no more."

"That'll be the day," Carl said. "My darling wife, would you like to dance?"

Geoff spun Sarah out on the dance floor as the ensemble segued from "Winter Wonderland" to "Jingle Bell Rock." Sarah estimated that there were about 80 people at the party, and more than half were dancing.

Sarah enjoyed the sheer pleasure of the motion for a few minutes, then said, "Did you know Teresa knew?"

"No," Geoff said. "I didn't think anyone did."

"Well, the mask is half off."

"If I get the job at Carsey-Mellon it'll be all the way off." He shrugged his shoulders as if a weight were lifting from them. "I can't even imagine what it'll be like just to talk about myself. I'm not into cruising or the bar scene — been there, done that — and I don't have many friends. And I can't make friends at work because I'm hiding all the time, telling near-lies all the time."

"I hate to tell you this," Sarah said into his ear as the music transitioned to the "Waltz of the Hours," "but I've been where you are, and once the closet door opens and you breathe in the fresh air there's no going back."

"I'm beginning to understand it," Geoff said. "How'd you get so wise?"

Sarah thought for a moment. "Privilege. I was in

an unassailable position. I had something no one could tarnish no matter what. And I hung out with women in the same position. So I'm not nearly as brave as I might seem. I was just lucky."

Geoff gazed down into her eyes. "I have a hard time believing that. So how did your parents take it? I haven't taken that step yet, either."

"Well, my mom freaked, but everything I did made her freak. She's very conscious of what others think, and she was concerned with what people thought of her because of me and felt that just about everything I did reflected badly on her."

"She's an 'enough about me, what do you think about me' kind of person?"

Sarah laughed into his chin. "Yes, that's it exactly. My dad, on the other hand, slapped me on the back, said whatever I did was okay by him and we haven't discussed it since."

"I could live with that," Geoff said.

"I can, too. But with my dad, well, it's hard to explain. He's an antiquities expert, and he does a lot of museum consulting and travel. He might drop in on me once a year. I always feel a little bit like he's just updating his note card on me. But he's affectionate. I know he loves me. He's just not a nurturer, no more than my mother is."

"So you got all your nurturing from your Grannie," Geoff said. "The world could use a lot of grannies."

"You said it." Sarah thought abruptly of Leslie, who was a born nurturer. The programmers, every one of them, loved her. As soon as they'd realized Matt was away, Leslie had been besieged with invitations for Christmas and New Year's Eve, and Sarah had overheard Gene trying to convince her to go to a hockey game. None of them could stand the idea of

Leslie being lonely or in need. Maybe she should invite Leslie to dinner some time next week. She missed Debra, missed her a lot. Maybe Leslie could come to mean what Debra had — everyone needed a best friend, or at least someone close who understood them.

She realized she wasn't thinking of Melissa as a best friend. She knew she should be alarmed, but she could not battle her way past the indifference she felt. She felt a chill run down her spine. It was almost as if she didn't like Melissa, which was absurd. She wouldn't have come to San Francisco if she didn't.

"Penny for them," Geoff said.

"Gathering wool," Sarah answered. "I'm getting hungry again."

"Allow me." Geoff pirouetted her off the dance floor and made an elaborate show of escorting her to the buffet table. He attentively plied her with food and drink until she surreptitiously threw a pea at him.

They danced until Sarah thought her feet would fall off. She had enjoyed herself too much to regret the blisters she later discovered when she stripped off her hose. She slipped into the bathtub for a good soak and wondered why Geoff hadn't met the right guy.

Everyone had a soulmate — Grannie MacNeil said it was true, and Sarah realized she still believed it, even though she'd been disillusioned. Maybe she hadn't given Melissa the chance to connect with her. Their physical relationship was too great to give up. You can't make dreams come true by wishing, Sarah told herself. When Melissa returned, she'd welcome her home with open arms, and an open heart.

* * * * *

Leslie turned on her office lights and settled into
her comfortable desk chair. It was pouring rain
outside, and Sunday at home alone on such a dark
day was too much to handle. If it was going to rain,
she would work. Sorting résumés for the accountant
job was going to be fun. She was dying to hire
somebody, completely the opposite from how she had
felt looking at attorney résumés.

She kicked herself mentally — twice. She was not
going to think about attorneys, patents, sequin
dresses, archery, the Olympics, dancing or anything
else that might remotely make her think of Sarah. It
was a simple crush, that was all, and just as quickly
as it had been born, it would die again. She should
just give it some time.

She shook herself out of a daze just as her dream
lips were about to brush that sexy tattoo on Sarah's
back. She conceded that the tattoo was not sexy,
then the devil child inside her added, "But her back
sure as hell is."

Cross with herself, she took the sorted résumés
out to Melody's desk with instructions to arrange
interviews. And then, without really thinking about
it, she found herself at the file cabinet. Rationally,
she told herself that she had every right to look at
Sarah's personnel file. Rationally, she knew no one
could say anything about her turning on the copier
so she could study Sarah's résumé at home, when she
had the leisure time. After all, she'd just given up
some of her Sunday to work, so why not examine the
résumé in the comfort of her home if she so desired.
It was all very rational.

Nevertheless, she took extra pains to put the file

back exactly as she had found it, a little hidden by the one in front. She locked the file cabinet again, put the key exactly when Melody had last left it, then scurried into her office with the copy.

The windshield wipers said, "Dumb move dumb move dumb move," as she drove home. She felt as if she had trade secrets in her purse rather than a single sheet of paper she had every right to have.

She made herself a bowl of cereal for dinner, and picked up the résumé. She skipped over the CompuSoft work history. She knew everything she needed to know about Sarah as a co-worker. She was thorough, serious and intelligent. The education section provided more clues about Sarah the person. She'd started her graduate and law degrees at the University of Washington five years after graduating with a B.A. from the University of Southern California. NCAA Archery women's team captain for two of the four years at USC. And there it was — Sarah had been a member of the 3-woman U.S. Olympic Archery team in 1984 and 1988.

Wow, was all Leslie could think. Sarah liked movies, gardening, and had done a summer internship with the Human Rights Campaign Fund during law school. So Richard *had* known Sarah was gay when he hired her. Piffle, Leslie thought. Now she owed him an apology.

Feeling childish, she read through the résumé again. It's just a crush, she told herself. Just a crush. You have to get out more.

She was still telling herself that the following day when she pulled into the parking lot and saw Sarah's Jaguar pull in right after her. The rain was still steadily falling, though the wind had died down. She ran for the warehouse door and held it open for Sarah, who was right behind her.

"Oh, man," Sarah was gasping. "Is it pouring or what?"

"Pouring," Leslie agreed. "Why aren't you wearing rainboots?"

Sarah shook one running-shoe-clad foot. "I didn't know I was going to step in a puddle. I hate rainboots."

"And where is your coat, young lady?"

"As if it's cold outside," Sarah said. "It's just wet, and the umbrella took care of most of that."

"You sound just like Matt," Leslie said. "It's plenty cold out there."

"Hah! It's balmy." Sarah headed in the direction of her office.

"Something's balmy," Leslie muttered. See, she told herself. She irritates you sometimes. You can't possibly have a crush on someone who irritates you.

"I heard that," Sarah called. "Hey," she said, turning. "What are you doing Saturday night?"

There was a dull roar in Leslie's ears. "Nothing, why?"

"Come to dinner, we'll get a video. I'll make sure Melissa doesn't have her group over that night."

Leslie walked nonchalantly to her own office door. "Is this a pity dinner?"

"Yeah," Sarah said, grinning. "Eight o'clock, don't be late."

This serves me right, Leslie thought. It just serves me right. She pities me and now I'm going to have dinner and watch her and the gorgeous girlfriend of hers make goo-goo eyes at each other all night. Great, just great.

She was not going to apologize to Richard, not now. This was all his fault, bringing another lesbian into the company as if Leslie were made of steel. This was all his fault, and Sarah's too for being so

173

unbearably attractive. She was wearing that lavender and green sweater again, didn't she know it made her eyes turn completely violet?

Part of Leslie's mind was turning over the question of what to wear, and if she perhaps needed to shop for something casual Sarah hadn't seen yet. She didn't own that part of her mind — it was a rotten traitor to be planning which bra she would wear, and if she'd shave her legs.

She heard Sarah answer the phone — her low voice carried through the wall far too well. It just wasn't fair.

Richard came into her office and Leslie gave him her best evil look.

"What did I do?" Richard stopped as if Leslie had shot him, one hand over his heart.

"Nothing," Leslie said, glaring for all she was worth. It's all your fault, you little Ewok from hell.

Sarah looked up from her coffee as a yawning Melissa headed for the kitchen. "Watch out, the floor might still be damp."

Melissa paused at the edge of the carpet and studied the kitchen floor. "You could eat off this."

"When I scrub a floor it knows it's been scrubbed," Sarah said. "It's probably dry."

Melissa tiptoed to the coffeemaker and then joined Sarah at the table. "I forgot we had company tonight."

"I think you'll like Leslie." Sarah set aside the newspaper and admired the sight of Melissa in flannel pajamas. Her homecoming from Los Angeles had been memorable. "Her son is gone for the holidays and I think she's very lonely."

174

Melissa sighed with satisfaction after a swallow of coffee. "I keep forgetting Christmas is right around the corner."

"About Christmas," Sarah said.

"Do you have plans?" Melissa went back to the kitchen for more sugar.

"Well, I only have a couple of days vacation coming to me, but I think Richard is planning to give everyone one or two more days off as a bonus, so I think I could manage to take the whole week off. I was wondering — would you like to spend Christmas in the snow?"

"Skiing? I'd love to."

"Well, there is some skiing, but I was thinking more along the lines of a remote cabin in the Cascades — my grandmother's farm. I inherited it when she died. It's a very special place to me." Sarah had been thinking the plan over ever since her night with Geoff. She wanted to open her life to Melissa.

"A white Christmas would be fun. The only thing I've got going is my lunch with Shana Dawson on Monday, so we could leave any time after that. Whenever you can get off."

She'd heard all about Shana Dawson when Melissa had come home on Tuesday night, and she thought it was great that Melissa would be receiving real advice and encouragement from a professional. "Most likely not until Friday afternoon. I think if we get into Seattle by eight we can be at the cabin by midnight, weather permitting. If not, we'll stop off at a motel. I just want you to see it in the morning light. We'd come home sometime the following weekend, if you want to be gone that long."

"Sounds great. I guess I could be busy if I decide to go the executive producer route that Shana suggested for the grant project. I'm going to ask her

175

more about that at our lunch. It would be good experience, but I'm still unhappy about not changing the content like I want to."

Sarah was relieved that Shana Dawson's advice had made Melissa see that the experience would be beneficial. She dried her hands, then lassoed Melissa with the dishtowel. After a very thorough kiss she let her go.

"What was that for?" Melissa slipped her arms around Sarah's waist.

"That was just because," Sarah said.

"And you had no ulterior motives?" Melissa waggled her eyebrows.

"You have a dirty mind," Sarah said, with mock severity.

"Yes, I do. Remember when I said you'd scrubbed the kitchen floor so hard you could eat off it?"

Sarah nodded, bewildered by the change of subject.

"I think I'll prove it," Melissa finished, and she pulled a giggling Sarah to the floor.

9

You desire to embrace it, to caress it, to possess
it . . . (Henry James)

"I know you said I shouldn't bring anything, but I couldn't help myself," Leslie said.

Sarah took the box of Joseph Schmidt chocolates. "I've heard these are local treasures."

"Open it," Leslie urged.

"Wow," Sarah breathed. Inside were ornate tablespoons made of bittersweet and milk chocolate. "My cappuccino just got better. You really didn't have to, but thank you. Here, give me your coat. Hey, I like that sweater, is it new?"

Leslie nodded. "I was killing time at the mall."

Sarah gave Leslie the brief guided tour, then led the way to the kitchen where Melissa was busy tearing lettuce. After introductions, she offered Leslie a drink. "You're our second formal dinner guest."

"And this time I won't burn the rice," Melissa said. "Fortunately, Sarah's friend Geoff was a good sport."

"Geoff is always a good sport," Sarah said. "At least when he's dancing."

"Oh, Geoff is the one who plies you with wine and takes you dancing, right?" Leslie settled onto the stool next to the breakfast bar.

Sarah emerged with a cold bottle of white wine in one hand and a chilled goblet in the other. "Umm-hmmm. He's a bad influence. But I think if I had ever wanted to have some guy's babies, it would be Geoff's. You know what I mean?"

Melissa said no at the same time Leslie said yes and Sarah laughed. "We seem to have a difference of opinion."

"Since I have had a baby with a man, I do know what you mean," Leslie said.

"You know, I've never wanted to have babies, much less with a man," Melissa said. "I'm a real lesbian, through and through."

Sarah handed Leslie her wine as she said, "But there's a huge lesbian baby boom going on."

Melissa dumped the chopped bell pepper into the salad and turned her attention to dicing jicama. "Well, there are some people in the community who think that's a sell-out. That some women are using the sexual freedom that other people worked hard for to imitate heterosexual life."

"So?" Leslie was shrugging her shoulders. "Takes all kinds to make a world. You wouldn't believe the number of times perfectly rational women have gotten icky expressions when they find out I was married once upon a time. Like they never made a mistake."

"That's a pretty big mistake, wouldn't you say?"

Melissa added croutons to the salad and turned to Sarah. "Where are the tossing thingies?"

Sarah found the tongs in the drawer and handed them over to Melissa. She stole a glance at Leslie, hoping she wasn't offended by Melissa's outspokenness.

"Actually," Leslie said slowly, looking at Sarah, "it wasn't that big a mistake. Alan and I got along. We had a beautiful child, and I think we'd still be married if I hadn't been with women before we got married. I knew what I was missing, even though what I had with him wasn't bad."

Sarah realized that Melissa was looking at Leslie with something like condescension. She tried to lighten the air by saying, "Was that before or after you left the commune?"

To Sarah's relief, Leslie grinned. "After, long after. I only lived in the commune for two years. Then Richard and I split the scene, man, to do our own thing."

"What were you trying to do?" Melissa set the salad to one side and leaned against the counter.

"More than anything, we were trying to be flower children."

Sarah did a little quick time subtraction. "But — even if you joined the commune when you were seventeen or eighteen, that would be nineteen seventy-what?"

"It was in nineteen seventy-too-late," Leslie said. "Richie got in at the tail end of what he calls the real time, but I was just plain too late. All I'd ever wanted to be was a flower child. Paint my face, grow organic food, live in tune with mother nature. But by the time I found Nirvana it was being rezoned for condos."

"What happened to the dream?" Sarah peeked in the oven at the baking salmon.

"Disco," Leslie said promptly. "Actually, I left the commune because my lesbianism was rocking the boat."

"Isn't that typical," Melissa commented. "Is the salmon done?"

"Just about, a few more minutes." To Leslie, Sarah said, "I thought flower children were into free love."

"They were. My love wasn't free enough since I only wanted to sleep with women. I was ruining the seating chart." Leslie spoke lightly, with a touch of wistfulness.

Sarah sensed that Leslie had long since come to terms with what must have been a painful rejection. "If I'm not being too nosy, how did you end up married?"

"How did we get on this topic?" Leslie sipped her wine. "Oh yeah, you wanted to have Geoff's babies."

"I did not say that," Sarah said. She got the potholders and lifted the roasting pan out of the oven. "I only said —"

"I'm just teasing. Do you need help?"

"No, I've got it. Mel, could you put the trivet — right there is fine." She set the hot pan down and poked the salmon. It flaked perfectly at the ends.

"Smells wonderful," Leslie said, coming to the counter. "What else are we having?"

"Rice with chick peas and raisins, tossed salad, peach and ginger chutney, French bread, and chocolate cake for dessert," Melissa said, her tone as friendly as Sarah could have wished for.

Sarah continued to poke the salmon, making sure it was cooked in the center. Melissa's hand stroked her back, and it felt good. Maybe Mel was getting over her initial reaction to Leslie — she hadn't seemed to like her at first.

"Sounds delicious," Leslie said, moving back to the breakfast bar.

Sarah finished her inspection of the salmon. "All done. Let's eat."

They settled at the table and for a while talked about the food and the wine, then Melissa turned to Leslie. "So you haven't said how you ended up married."

Sarah wanted to kick her, but instead she said smoothly, "Maybe that's because I was being nosy."

"No, really, I don't mind talking about it. I got married because Alan asked me. It's as simple as that. We were married for seven years. I was the one who got the itch."

"Because he asked you?" Melissa put her hand briefly on Sarah's. "Darling, the salmon is perfect."

"Well, we met in the commune, and every couple of months after I left, Alan would drop into my life for a few days, just to catch up, chill out, all that jazz. Our relationship was friendship only, and out of the blue he asked me to marry him. He knew I preferred women. I knew I preferred women."

"How could you do it?" Melissa looked incredulous.

Leslie shot a glance at Sarah, then said, "I wanted a home. I wanted a family. It was only . . . oh, sixteen years ago, but the only way to have those things was the regular heterosexual way. I was twenty-three, the bank had just foreclosed on the organic farm Richard and I were running, and I wanted to succeed at something, so why not succeed in creating a family? I'd always known I wanted kids.

181

I wanted a house overflowing with them. My own commune, you know?"

"Before I started teaching my archery class, I wouldn't have understood in the least. But now — I can sort of see it. Kids are not space aliens to me anymore."

"How many kids do you have?" Melissa pushed back her chair. "I'll get the wine."

"Just the one. Turned out my ovaries had other ideas. Just after Matt turned two, I told Alan I couldn't go on. He wasn't surprised. He's remarried now, has two more boys, and I think we both look back at the time we were married with some fondness. Our only regret — if we have any — is how Matt might have been damaged by our lack of foresight."

Melissa topped off Sarah's glass, then Leslie's. After she had reseated herself, she put her hand on Sarah's again.

"He didn't seem damaged to me," Sarah said. "I'm a child of divorce. No, it wasn't easy sometimes to understand my parents' behavior, but I know they still loved me."

"Alan and I tried our best to make Matt feel like he had two homes where he was equally loved. I can't speak ill of Alan. I know that's not the party line. We loved each other," Leslie continued. "But it wasn't —" Sarah saw Leslie's gaze settle briefly on Melissa's fingers entwining with Sarah's. "Well, you know what it wasn't." She winked at Sarah knowingly.

"That I do," Sarah said. She squeezed Melissa's fingers.

"Pity is," Leslie went on, "I've found women who

made my body go ka-thump-thump, which is what I was longing for all the time I was with Alan, but never one who made me feel the way Alan did in all the other ways. He was . . . comfortable."

"I've never heard comfortable included on the list of what makes a perfect romance," Melissa said.

"If it's not on the list, it should be," Leslie said. "There's a time when you stop wondering what the other person is thinking and you just know. It's comfortable. I'm probably fooling myself that I'll ever find the ka-thump-thump and the comfort in the same woman."

The doorbell rang and Sarah started to push back her chair.

"I'll get it," Melissa said.

Sarah looked after Melissa for a moment, then turned to Leslie. "I don't think you're wrong to want both."

"I can see that," Leslie said. "She's very nice."

"Thanks." Sarah didn't know what else to say.

Melissa returned with a file folder. "Just Leeza dropping something off for me."

"Sarah told me you're making a documentary," Leslie said. Sarah heard the distinct sound of the subject being changed. Leslie must have felt as if she were being interrogated.

"Yes, I am." Melissa brightened. "I've hit a kind of a funding snag, but I'm sure it will all work out. I was in L.A. this past weekend and I met an agent, Shana Dawson. She's the agent for that lesbian who mortgaged everything she owned to make *Dream Shadow*. Did you see it?"

"I — well, it wasn't my cup of tea," Leslie said. "But it was good to see someone making a romantic film about lesbians."

"Well, Shana knows everyone in L.A. She knew exactly the bind I was in with my grant."

"Which is?" Leslie seemed genuinely interested, and Sarah relaxed.

"Here, let me take the plates," Sarah said. "You guys talk and I'll listen as I clear up."

"Thank you," Leslie said as Sarah picked up her plate. "It was so much better than the bowl of Cheerios I had last night."

"You're welcome. I'll bring in the cake after I take care of these. A dishwasher would be nice, but I've gotten used to hot soapy water. There's something therapeutic about washing dishes."

"You haven't washed enough of them," Leslie said.

Sarah cleaned up the kitchen and didn't contribute much to the conversation. She watched Leslie and Melissa talk and heaved a sigh of relief. It was important that they like each other because Sarah liked them both. She had been particularly anxious that Leslie take Melissa seriously, in exactly the way Debra had not. She didn't know why it was so important to her, but it was. Leslie looked truly interested, and Sarah smiled into the soap suds.

Leslie longed for a conversational opening to offer to dry the dishes while Sarah washed. She wanted to talk to Sarah, not to her girlfriend. Melissa was explaining how she'd met Shana Dawson in the hotel hot tub during the conference. Leslie was amazed that, based on one conversation, Melissa was ready to throw over her grant on the Jacuzzi-induced promise of some entertainment agent.

Maybe it would work out for Melissa, but Leslie

had her doubts. She wondered if Sarah had doubts. She must, Leslie thought. She's too down-to-earth.

She let Melissa prattle on about the other people she'd met in the hot tub and seminars. *I'll bet this cures me of my crush.* If Sarah is ocean-deep and complicated how can she be head over heels for this — well, Melissa wasn't precisely a bimbo, but she seemed so young, and a lot of her politics were so ... seventies. But she was *not* in Sarah's league.

Slow down, Leslie told herself in her most stern tone. Just slow down. Melissa was not her girlfriend. Sarah was not her girlfriend. Maybe Melissa was just a late starter. And she did have dreams. Maybe they weren't that realistic, but neither were some of Leslie's in the end. Give her a chance.

She'd be more inclined to give Melissa a chance if she hadn't made that nasty crack about being a "real" lesbian, "through and through," as if the millions of lesbians who slept with men and had children by them or other means weren't really lesbians. How shallow could you get?

"So I think I might be able to get Shana to represent me — sell my novels. She seemed very interested and she's sold lesbian novels to the really big publishing houses. I need to follow up, so I'm going to fly down for the day on Monday and have lunch with her. She gave me her assistant's number, and we're all set."

"I'm almost done, so prepare for cake," Sarah said from the kitchen. "Is your grant going to cover the airfare again?"

"Airfare is really cheap to L.A. if you book the tickets right. And I've got plenty of grant money to play with."

As if it's Monopoly money, Leslie thought.

"Aren't they going to want it all back?" Sarah came in from the kitchen with a cake box and dessert plates. The sputtering sound of the cappuccino machine nearly drowned out her words.

"I don't think so," Melissa said. "After all, I have done part of the project, and I'd be more than willing to give someone all the notes and my exhibit listings. And Shana said maybe I don't have to give it up at all, but contract with someone else to do it. I'd be like the executive producer. Maybe Janica would like to finish it, though she's a little bit radical at times."

"I was going to put this on a plate," Sarah said, gesturing at the pink box, "but then I thought you both might prefer to watch me undress it." She winked at Leslie.

"Let me guess," Leslie said. "It's chocolate."

"Chocolate is such an inadequate description of this cake," Sarah said. She slowly opened the box, then popped the tape on the sides. With a dramatic gesture, she exposed the cake. "Tah-dah!"

I might not be over my crush after all, she thought. The cake wasn't just chocolate. It was chocolate on chocolate on chocolate with chocolate on top. The kind of cake a person could use to seduce Counselor Troi — or any chocolate lover for that matter. Sarah was inhaling deeply.

"I have had a chocolate craving for the past week," Sarah said. "This ought to satisfy it."

"A little piece for me. I'm trying to lose five pounds." Melissa put her hand on her stomach, which Leslie thought was already plenty flat.

Give me a break, Leslie thought. "So am I," she said. "I want a piece like Melissa's, except three times bigger."

Sarah laughed. "I'll get the cappuccino, oh, and those chocolate spoons you brought, Les." She was back in just a moment with frothy mugs and the box of chocolates.

Leslie sighed in bliss as she swallowed the first bite. "I think I'll wake up from the sugar coma sometime on Tuesday."

"It is good," Melissa said. She passed on having a chocolate spoon with her coffee but accepted another slim slice of cake at Sarah's urging.

Sarah settled back into her seat and Leslie watched her swoon as she tasted the cake. Then she slowly stirred her cappuccino with a chocolate spoon, scooped up some of the whipped cream on the coffee and put the spoon in her mouth, closing her eyes briefly. "God, this is divine."

"Almost as good as sex?" Melissa was gazing at Sarah with an indulgent smile and Leslie suddenly wanted to slap her.

"Almost . . ." Sarah was grinning back at Melissa and Leslie suddenly wanted to slap her too. What was it about Sarah that brought out her baser instincts? She'd been thinking nonstop about sex for the past week. Primal, honest-to-God, jungle fever, ripped clothes, heart-pounding, hold on for dear life, sweaty and breathless, ride 'em cowboy sex, sex, sex.

Maybe she was having early menopause. She felt as if she were running a fever, all the time. And watching Sarah have chocolate orgasms was not helping. Watching Melissa touch Sarah for what seemed like the hundredth time was not helping. Her bra and panties feeling two sizes too small was not helping.

Nothing was going to help, Leslie realized. She was stuck until this thing ran its course. Her priority was keeping her feelings from Sarah.

So she smiled, she laughed, she asked questions about Melissa's novels and tried very hard to be the perfect guest. The façade slipped a little when Melissa began describing what she planned for her next novel — or screenplay. She hadn't made up her mind.

"I want to write about the real courage that the activists have. Actually, it was an idea for a short story that Shana Dawson liked, about the first time a woman walks down the street with a DYKE sticker on her jacket. That just seems so brave to me. And there are lots of other stories like that. Shana thought it might make a great short film too."

"That sounds interesting," Leslie said, and in fact it did. "I know the two women who made their auto roadside service club give them joint membership."

"That's not quite what I had in mind," Melissa said. "It doesn't seem like the same thing."

"Oh," Leslie said, blinking. What was the difference? "How about a woman coming out at a PTA meeting?"

Melissa shrugged. "I was thinking more of the physical, day-to-day, in-your-face activism. Loud and proud courage that makes people stop and think about their prejudices."

Leslie bit back her retort. She wanted to explain to Melissa that the other people in the PTA had thought Leslie was being very "in their face" by just mentioning her sexuality in passing, and they'd said as much. Continuing to go to the meetings when she was greeted with coldness, if not outright rudeness, was one of the hardest things she'd ever done — she hated conflict.

She tried to find some common ground. "I do know what you mean, and I am often amazed at how brave some people are — particularly some of the young women. They are very courageous, and I admire them. They are making change by being, as you say, loud and proud. But . . . well, society changes slowly, and it's rare when just one type of pressure effects all the necessary change. So it takes other kinds of courage, and other kinds of activism, to change everything, for everyone."

Sarah was nodding. "When the English wanted to finish their conquest of Wales, they outlawed the language, even in the churches. There's a lot of Welsh history about the big heroes — both Llewellyns, in particular, and many of the warlords. Owen Glendower even shows up in Shakespeare. But I've always thought that mothers who covertly taught their children Welsh, and the storytellers who kept the stories of their country alive in their own language, and the priests who continued to have secret services in Welsh — I've always thought they were heroes too. Very quiet heroes."

"I see what you mean," Melissa said. "I'll have to think about it."

"There are two women in L.A. who won a settlement against a restaurant that refused to seat them in the 'romantic' section because they were two women. I always thought that it was a pretty amazing thing that they went to court over something so small, but the policy completely invalidated them as a couple. They said it was the little things that kept us from being equal."

Melissa just smiled and sipped her coffee, and Leslie could tell she wasn't impressed. She wondered if Melissa would think Rosa Parks was as brave as the Selma marchers. She felt tired — and old. Melissa looked like she might be almost 30, and the 9 years between them were looming pretty big. Melissa hadn't been out in the world enough to see how today fits into yesterday fits into tomorrow.

Her peevishness faded as she finished the cake. Chocolate cures all things, she thought. She glanced at Sarah, felt the familiar jolt in her nether regions and knew there was one thing chocolate wasn't curing.

"My parents would be so amazed if I actually got an agent," Melissa was saying. "They've been after me for years to get a so-called real job, as if what I'm trying to do isn't real. They think it's a phase, just like being a lesbian. I got a letter from them today, Sare, I forgot to tell you. They sent me a plane ticket to come home to Cambridge for Christmas."

"Oh," Sarah said, blankly. "I thought we were going to the farm —"

"Don't worry," Melissa said, "I'm not going. They'll just spend the entire time pressuring me to get a Master's in something, anything. They send a ticket every year and every year I cash it in. I don't know what I'll do with the cash."

Flibbertigibbet. Leslie congratulated herself on finally finding the word she'd been searching for. Melissa was a flibbertigibbet, and although it was certainly none of her business, and she would never dream of giving Sarah advice on her love life, she just didn't see what Sarah saw in Melissa. She seemed like all glitter and no substance.

Sarah laughed at something Melissa said, that lovely, easy laugh of hers, and Melissa leaned over to kiss Sarah lightly on the lips. Leslie saw the flame leap in Sarah's eyes, and her stomach turned over. She knew what Sarah saw in Melissa, all right. The sex was probably fantastic. Melissa was all glitter and no substance. She bit back a giggle — the chocolate had gone right to her head.

She left as soon as she could decently do so, but late enough to make it appear she had thoroughly

190

enjoyed herself, and she mostly had. Except for any part of the evening that involved Melissa.

You're just jealous, she chided herself. There's nothing wrong with Melissa, you just want there to be. Grow up. And get over this crush, because nothing good is going to come of it. Nothing good at all.

"Thanks for dinner, it was fun."

Sarah looked up from her monitor and smiled a welcome to Leslie. "It was my pleasure. Believe me, the food has rarely been that good — the cake was insurance."

"I had chocolate dreams," Leslie said. She leaned against Sarah's desk.

"What are you working on so intently?"

"Why, I'm doing completely personal work on company time, of course. I'm changing the car rental for our trip to my grandmother's farm."

"Is this the farm you're always talking about?"

"I am not always talking about it," Sarah said. "Only when appropriate."

"Like telling Mark he didn't know what shit work was until he'd scrubbed a hen roost?"

"He was whining," Sarah said, aware that Leslie was teasing her.

"And comparing gardening tips with Richard? Let's see, I do believe you were comparing the efficacy of fertilizer during our last group lunch."

"Sorry," Sarah mumbled. "I didn't mean to put you off your feed."

"I'm teasing —"

"I know —"

"So have a great time."

"What did you end up deciding to do?" Sarah knew that Richard had invited Leslie to go with him to a friend's for the holiday.

"I'll probably go with Richard. But four days of listening to bootleg live Grateful Dead recordings and being stoned most of the time — and eating like a horse, of course — it just doesn't have the appeal it used to. But it is in Stinson Beach."

"Hmm. Mixed blessings."

"But I'll have fun. I don't want to stay home because I'll just mope, and there's nothing so pressing here that I want to come to work —"

A burst of music interrupted Leslie, and Sarah looked at her with eyebrows raised. Someone was playing "Jingle Bells" very loudly. Leslie just grinned and yelled, "Santa's here," over the racket.

Sarah signed offline and followed Leslie to the newly completed video production area. Most of the programmers were already there, and she stopped short at the sight of Richard in a Santa suit. It was perfect casting.

"Ho, ho, ho," Richard was chanting. "Is everyone here? Okay, cut the music." He was standing on the stage, which was the only way for him to be taller than anyone else. "The holidays are coming early this year because we're ahead of schedule on everything. Gene and I have conferred and we believe that our delivery date for beta testing can be moved from next October to next March."

The programmers let out a cheer. Richard called for quiet again. "Leslie and I are so confident that what we're creating is going to take the video development world by storm that we're giving everyone one hundred shares of stock as a holiday bonus — wait, wait — and, even better I'm sure you'll all agree — two weeks off, starting next Monday. With pay, of course. Thank you, everybody, for working so hard this year!"

There was the sound of a cork popping and Sarah saw Gene wave a champagne bottle. "To the best programming staff in the world!"

Someone turned the music back up and Sarah wanted to bolt out and finish her vacation reservations. Two whole weeks off — she and Melissa could stay the entire week at Grannie MacNeil's. And a hundred more shares of stock, that was an unbelievable bonus. She'd done some research on stock prices for companies like MagicWorks, and there was potential for the price to inflate 10 to 20 times. The hundred shares extra could end up being almost a year's salary.

Richard was dancing The Pony with Leslie. Their image was up on the big video screen. Sarah went over to Mark, who was acting as cameraman. "I didn't know this was working." Mark swiveled the camera toward Sarah, and she saw herself on the big screen. "Stop that," she ordered him.

"We're all tired of doing work on videos of ourselves. Do some Perry Mason talk."

She put her hands on her hips and pursed her lips. "I'm not a litigator. And if you don't stop filming me, I'll habeas your corpus."

"Conga line," someone shouted and the next thing Sarah knew she was being swept into the line. Somehow they managed to do a conga beat to "Holiday Hootenanny." These people are nuts, she thought.

The line turned on itself and Sarah high-fived Leslie as she went by. But, she added to herself, it's a nice kind of nuts.

10

An arrow for the heart like a sweet voice.
(Lord Byron)

Sarah was glad she'd told Melissa she would stay at work until Melissa's flight came in. ˙She needed the extra hour and a half to drink some coffee — Richard's celebratory champagne had been potent.

The warehouse was quiet, for once. Everyone had gone home on a wave of good cheer. It was funny, she thought, how much she had come to like working in a small company. The holiday parties at Compu-Soft were certainly splashy enough, but beyond a general drunkenness, there wasn't a lot of cheer. What MagicWorks' party had lacked in caviar had been more than offset by spontaneity. Richard had put company resources into what people really wanted — time off and extra income.

She wasn't too muzzy to finish arranging for an all-weather rental vehicle, complete with chains and a cellular phone, just in case. She was just signing off the rental agency's Web page when she heard the Jaguar's horn outside.

She hurried out to greet Melissa, who was getting out of the driver's seat. "No, you drive," Sarah said. "I'm still a bit tipsy from our party. Richard gave everybody two weeks off for the holidays."

"That's great," Melissa said, her gray eyes lighting up. "I have some marvelous news, just unbelievable news, and if you get some time off — it's perfect."

Sarah cajoled and pleaded for more details, even attempted a freeway seduction, but Melissa was adamant. She was expecting a message on the machine at home, and if the message was good, then she would tell Sarah all the news.

Melissa raced up the stairs ahead of her and as Sarah came in the door, she heard an unknown woman's voice on the answering machine saying, "Everything was a go."

Melissa gave a whoop of joy and flew to the door to hug Sarah. "Okay, okay, I'll tell you now." She pulled Sarah into the living room and pushed her down onto the sofa.

"Shana Dawson is going to be my agent," she said with a million-gigawatt smile.

"Darling, that's terrific," Sarah said, both amazed and thrilled. No wonder Melissa looked as if she'd won the lottery.

"There's more. The phone message meant that she was able to get invitations for you and me to go to a really, I mean, really swank New Year's Eve party where everyone who is anyone in the lesbian and gay community will be."

"Is the party in Los Angeles?" Sarah realized she'd have to modify the return flight, but there was only a small fee to change the tickets.

"Of course," Melissa said. "And guess what else? She also got us an invitation to a Christmas Eve party in Hollywood. The woman who made *Dream Shadow* will be there."

Christmas Eve. "So you want to spend Christmas week in L.A.," Sarah said slowly. She tried to keep the disappointment out of her voice.

"Not just the week, silly! Shana says that there's something going on all the time in L.A. It's just not like here. She can get me entrance to a zillion parties and symposiums, I just have to be ready to go where she says. If you have two weeks off we'll have plenty of time to find an apartment before you give notice. I mean, if you give notice now they won't let you have the time off, will they?"

"An apartment," Sarah repeated, feeling stupid. She just wasn't tracking what Melissa was saying.

"Well, we'll need someplace to live, won't we? I told Shana that you found a job here really easily, and she says that the Valley is full of software firms."

"I lucked into this job," Sarah managed to say. "Melissa, I —"

"Isn't this the best news?" Melissa sank down onto the sofa next to Sarah. "You are happy, aren't you?"

"I'm delighted for you." Sarah groped for words. Her head throbbed as if a giant gong had gone off inside her skull.

"This is really going to lead somewhere, instead of this dead-end grant. I'm going to resign it. It's just not worth my time."

I don't love her enough to do this again. The

realization came to Sarah on the heels of a wave of nausea. "I can't —" She swallowed, hard. "I can't go with you."

"What? Next week? Oh, you wanted to go to that farm place. I'm sorry, darling. Maybe we can go the week after New Year's."

"No, I mean I can't go with you to L.A. to live."

Melissa's glow faded. "But I'm sure you could get another job."

"I don't want to find another job," Sarah said. "I can't move again so soon. It'll look flaky. And I made a commitment to MagicWorks to do their patent application. I've only done about a quarter of the job. I can't just bail out on my archery students, either. Not when . . . after L.A., where? Will you go to New York? Chicago?"

Melissa's chin quivered. After a long silence, she said, "I guess, well, I understand about your not wanting to leave your job. Well, airfare is cheap," she said, more brightly. "Shana did mention that she's got an in-law cottage at her place I could stay in until I can afford a place of my own."

Sarah had to consciously stop herself from base speculations about exactly where Melissa would be staying. It wasn't the point. Melissa was not getting the point. "That's great," she said, feeling hollow. "But I'm not sure there's any point in my visiting you." She took a deep, shaky breath.

"What are you saying? That if I go to L.A. we're through?"

"I'm not giving you an ultimatum," Sarah said, shaking her head. "I know you're going to go. It was inevitable, and I've only just realized it. But I wasn't cut out to be a gypsy."

"You never really believed I'd make something of myself, did you?" Melissa jammed her hands in her pockets. "I was just a great fuck to you all along, wasn't I?"

Sarah frowned to hold back her tears. "If I hadn't believed in you, I would never have moved here. It wasn't easy for me to do."

"And you've been bottling up all that resentment, and I get all of it out of the blue like this? How mature is that?"

"Oh God, Melissa, I don't want to fight. I don't want to do this." Sarah's shoulders ached, and she realized she wasn't breathing enough. "I haven't resented it. I thought I was investing in something . . . permanent. I am very happy here. I love my job, I like this apartment — but God, Mel, you can't expect me to pull up my stakes again so fast. I can't believe that you know so little about me that you'd think I could do it. And I've just realized that I knew so little about you that I didn't see this coming. Under- neath the passion — we're strangers. And we won't stop being strangers if we have to get on planes to see each other."

Melissa was blinking back tears. "If you loved me, you wouldn't do this."

"Do what?" Sarah's voice broke, and she didn't bother to hold back the tears anymore. "And I could say exactly the same thing."

"Then what's the point?"

"There is no point. That's the point." She wiped her cheeks with hands that trembled.

Melissa's lips twisted, but she managed to say, "I think I'll use my parents' plane ticket money to buy a car and I'll get out of your hair. You can't get anywhere in L.A. without a car. And I think I'll spend the night at Janica's."

Sarah held her head in her hands after Melissa

left. She was beyond tears. A crushing weariness made it hard to move. She kept replaying the scene with Melissa in her head. It just didn't seem possible for her hopes and dreams to have dissolved so quickly, like a snowman in the rain.

Melissa would come back — surely she would come back. Sarah went to the window, just as if she expected to see Melissa coming back up the stairs, even though she knew Melissa wouldn't be there. And if Melissa came back, she would just leave again.

The phone rang and she automatically answered it. A woman asked to speak to Melissa.

Sarah answered automatically. "I'm sorry, but Melissa isn't in at the moment. May I take a message?"

"This must be Sarah — it's Molly. How are you?"

"Fine, and you?"

"Peachy. Is Mel still in L.A.?"

"I should see her tomorrow," Sarah answered.

"Oh," Molly said, sounding a little puzzled. "Well, I'll give her a call then. Nothing important. You know, Sarah, while I have you . . ."

"Yes?"

"I think it's really great what you're doing for Mel. She's very creative, but she needs someone like you to keep her on the planet, know what I mean?"

"Sure," Sarah said, having no idea what Molly meant.

"It isn't every aspiring artist who has someone with the means to let them be free."

"That's me," Sarah said, trying to laugh. "Patron of the arts."

"Well, you're more than that to Mel, I'm sure. Anyway, I have to run. Just tell her I called."

"Will do," Sarah said. She hung up the phone and

sank against the wall, slowly sliding to the floor. She wrapped her arms around her knees and bowed her head. The phone rang again, but she made no move to answer it. The answering machine whirred, then she listened to a jubilant Geoff announcing that he had gotten the job at Carsey-Mellon.

Well, at least someone was having a happy Christmas.

She had no idea how long she sat there, her mind a blank, but a bout of shivers got her back on her feet and into a hot shower.

She dried the shower wall, folded the towel neatly on the bar, brushed her teeth, flossed, brushed out her hair, slipped into a nightshirt, folded back the covers and turned out the lights, all the while feeling like a sleepwalker. She didn't think she would sleep, but she was shocked awake by her alarm what seemed like minutes later.

She knew she couldn't face the day. Everyone at work would be talking about what they were going to do with their two weeks and Sarah could barely conceptualize the next two hours. The future just didn't seem real.

"Sarah's got a head cold, and I scheduled both your finalists to see Richard tomorrow." Melody handed Leslie a plastic-wrapped bundle. "And my mom made these."

"Ooo, gingerbread cookies," Leslie said. She quickly bit the head off the cookie on top. "Did Sarah call?"

"Yeah, and she sounded really congested and miserable."

Leslie hmphed. "I hope it's not too serious."

"I'm sure you'll be able to render TLC if necessary." Melody snickered.

"You're impertinent today, aren't you?" Leslie glared at her, then headed for her office.

"Hey, I'm a shareholder in this company," Melody said, hands on her hips. "Show some respect."

"Yeah, yeah, yeah," Leslie muttered as she set her backpack down. She chomped on a gingerbread leg and wondered if Sarah was okay. Well, if she wasn't, the lovely and talented Melissa would be there to render comfort. Get on with your work, she admonished herself.

But concentration eluded her. She had nothing terribly pressing on her desk except for the accounting stuff. And if Richard liked the two people she'd found she wouldn't have to do it — so why start? With the entire office shutting down in just four more days it was hard to get up a head of steam on something.

She ambled over to Richard's office to ask about the moved-up timelines for releasing a beta version of Motion. Richard wasn't there, and Gene's office was also unoccupied.

This is pretty sad, she thought. Surely she could get through a single day without Sarah nearby.

By noon she was ferociously bored, so she went to her favorite drive-thru and then headed for the nearest mall. She bought herself a new pair of black jeans and then acquired a gigantic box of See's candy for the office. She'd make sure something was left for Sarah, provided she was back to work tomorrow.

And if Sarah wasn't back, Leslie didn't know how she'd get through the day. Which, all in all, she told herself, was pretty damned pathetic.

* * * * *

"Your nose is as red as a cranberry, girl."

Sarah smiled wanly at Melody. "I don't think I'm contagious." She had found maintaining the fiction of a head cold more convenient than the truth.

"I hope not, I'm going whale watching next week. Christmas in Mendocino. I don't need a cold."

"Where's Mendocino?"

"Up the coast about three hours or so. It's a nice, little artisty type place. I'm taking my mom. She hasn't had a proper vacation in three years."

"Well, aren't you a good daughter," Sarah said. "I didn't even send my mom a Christmas card."

Melody gave her a stern look. "That karma will come back to bite you in the butt."

"Yeah, probably," Sarah said. She sniffed and blotted her nose. Maybe if she'd just let herself have a good, long cry, she wouldn't be so weepy.

Melody's phone rang, and Sarah turned gratefully to her office. Making conversation was so difficult, and so tiring. She settled at her desk, wiped her nose, then fumbled in her satchel for the full box of tissues she'd brought.

"Hey, you're back."

Sarah straightened and smiled as much as she was able to at Leslie. For a moment she wanted to tell her everything, but she just couldn't. She couldn't tell anyone what an idiot she had been. Melissa had emptied the apartment of her belongings yesterday afternoon and that was that. She was gone. She was not coming back. Sarah had found herself wondering if Melissa would have waited a week if she'd known her birthday/Christmas present was to have been a computer.

Cynicism and anger just made her feel worse.

"But I don't think you're a hundred percent," Leslie said. "Earth to Sarah."

"Sorry. I'm functional, just a little slow."

"Decongestants do that to me too." Leslie put a paper towel on Sarah's desk. "This will make you feel better."

"Chocolates," Sarah said, finding a little enthusiasm from somewhere. "You're a good woman."

"There was a huge box yesterday, which is long gone, but I saved these for you. I've always found that a Bordeaux and a cup of tea is downright medicinal. I can get you the tea now."

Sarah blinked back tears. Leslie's kindness was melting her resolve to keep her anguish to herself. She wiped her nose and said, "Maybe later. I'm not sure I'm going to make it all day, anyway."

"You don't look like you could turn on your computer, much less type."

"I feel like a popped balloon," Sarah admitted. "But I've got my archery class this afternoon, and it's the last one of the year. I've got presents for the kids, so I'm going to try to stick it out."

"You poor thing," Leslie said. "Well, if you want any tea and aspirin, you know where to find it."

"Thanks, Mom," Sarah said.

Leslie smiled brightly and, much to Sarah's relief, left without another word.

Leslie was glad to see Sarah looking a little more alive on Thursday. She was still red-nosed and bleary-eyed, but at least she was walking around at her normal pace, and she seemed able to follow a conversation. With any luck at all, she wouldn't call Leslie "Mom" anymore. Her feelings were far from maternal.

The day was winding down when she realized she

hadn't heard Sarah laugh all day. Nor had she been talking much at all. Maybe she had a sore throat, Leslie speculated. Unable to help herself, she decided to do a "mom" thing.

"You still look like you could use this." She set the cup of chamomile tea down on Sarah's desk. "And I've got one last Bordeaux."

"That's sweet, no pun intended," Sarah said. "Thanks."

"Are you feeling better?"

"Uh-huh." Sarah sipped the tea and smiled somewhat in her usual way.

She's lying, Leslie suddenly thought. And that smile is a fake. But whatever it is, she's not talking, so leave her alone. "That's good. You wouldn't want to be sick for the holidays."

Sarah's eyes turned a shadowy blue, then she lowered her gaze to the tea mug. "I'm sure I'll be over this by then."

Back in her office, Leslie decided to clean out her middle desk drawer. It was mindless, and she needed to think. Something was wrong with Sarah. Leslie puzzled over the few clues she had while she sorted her vast collection of paperclips and pens. Everyone accused her of walking off with their pens.

Well, the problem couldn't be Melissa — they had been the picture of happiness on Saturday. Even if they'd had a fight, it wouldn't have put Sarah in that condition. A death in the family? Well, then why wouldn't she just say so? A head cold did seem the most likely explanation, but Leslie wasn't buying it.

She had made neat piles of the different-sized clips, when she heard Sarah leaving. Her curiosity got the better of her, and she hurried out of the building after her. The cold wind made her wish she'd brought her coat.

"Hey, Sarah!" She rubbed her arms and hurried toward Sarah. "I have a quick question."

Sarah turned back. The knife-edged wind caught her hair and blew it into her eyes. She brushed it back as she walked toward Leslie. "Where's your jacket, young lady?"

"Yeah, yeah, yeah," Leslie said. "Have you done contracts for outside consultants?"

Sarah blinked. "Yes."

"Well, when you get in tomorrow, maybe we could talk a little bit about it. With the new timeline for beta testing I should be thinking about hiring technical writers, and they'll need nondisclosure agreements."

"Sure," Sarah said. She sniffed. The wind was further reddening her nose and ears. "How about over that first cup of coffee?"

"Great," Leslie said. "Give my regards to Melissa. When does your plane leave tomorrow?"

Sarah's mouth opened as if she were going to answer, and then she stopped.

Leslie put her hand on Sarah's arm. "What's really wrong?"

A tear gathered in the corner of one murky blue-violet eye. Sarah whispered something, but the wind snatched it away.

"What?" Leslie leaned closer, and she felt Sarah's arm tremble under her hand.

"She left me."

"Oh, my God," Leslie breathed. Anger exploded right behind her eyes and she literally saw red. That little bitch. "She left you? How could she leave you?"

"Easily. Without a glance backward." Sarah's voice was far too calm and it chilled Leslie in places the wind couldn't reach.

"Stay right here," she said firmly. "I'll be right back."

She flew back into the building, passed a startled Melody and scrabbled up her belongings from behind her desk. She dashed into the Cave to find Angie, who biked to work and lived just a few miles from Leslie.

Angie was just strapping on her helmet.

"Angie, do me a favor, would you?"

"Sure, Les."

Leslie handed Angie the keys to her car. "Could you drive my car home? I don't want to leave it in the lot — Sarah's feeling a lot worse and her girl-friend is out of town, and I don't want to leave her alone, so I'm going to take her to my place until she feels better. And if my Volvo's not safe in the lot overnight, her car certainly isn't."

"No problem. I wasn't looking forward to the entire ride anyway — not with that wind. I'll drop it off at your house and ride home from there. It's all downhill."

"You're a peach," Leslie said over her shoulder.

She dashed past Melody again. "Tell Richard I'm canceling dinner. And don't say another word," she admonished. "Not a word." She stopped just inside the warehouse door, took a deep breath, then made a calm exit.

Sarah was standing where Leslie had left her, though with her jacket unzipped she must have been freezing. She didn't say anything as Leslie approached.

"Give me your car keys."

She handed them over wordlessly.

"I'm going to take you back to my place. I think you could use a long soak in a hot tub."

Sarah slid into the passenger seat without a sound, and buckled up when Leslie told her to.

Leslie studied the instrumentation on the dash, then decided she would not think about how expensive the car was. It had a steering wheel and four tires, just like any other car. She looked for the keyhole on the steering column, then the dash, but couldn't find it.

"Sarah, help me out."

Sarah stirred, then pointed at the console dividing their seats. The keyhole was just in front of the gear shift.

"I'd have never found it. Well, here we go."

She managed to back out without damaging anything, and just a few minutes later she was competently negotiating the short freeway trip down 101 to her exit. She was used to the Volvo's slower reflexes, but Sarah didn't say anything when Leslie stomped on the brakes to avoid a truck and nearly put them both through the windshield.

She slipped the Jaguar into the Volvo's usual parking place in the garage, then navigated the numb Sarah through the house to Matt's bedroom. She returned in a few minutes with an extra swimsuit.

"This is going to be too big for you, but it'll preserve your modesty."

"What's this for?" Sarah hadn't even taken off her jacket.

"Hot tub. It'll do you a world of good. I'm going to make a couple of sandwiches."

She shut the door to the bedroom behind her and hoped Sarah would continue to respond to her suggestions. She turned on the Jacuzzi jets and took off the cover triggered the furnace and went to the kitchen. Sarah was obviously in shock, and Leslie was willing to bet she hadn't eaten since — Tuesday, when she'd called in sick. Leslie mentally reviewed all the synonyms she knew for *bitch* as she spread mustard on bread.

Sarah appeared a few minutes later. The part of Leslie that never behaved appropriately in any situation hooted at the sight of Sarah in a swimsuit, but Leslie gave it a smack on the butt and sent it to its room without supper. "There are towels in the cupboard right next to the hot tub, and robes on the hooks. Through that door, then up the stairs." Leslie pointed. "I'll be right out with sandwiches after I change."

She heard Sarah sliding into the water and finished making the sandwiches. She changed quickly into her own suit — which hadn't been used since Matt left — grabbed a couple of peach Snapples and joined Sarah.

Sarah was waist deep in the bubbling water. Leslie handed her half of a sandwich. "Eat fast or it'll get soggy and taste like chlorine."

To her relief, Sarah complied, then accepted the Snapple, then the other half of the sandwich. The hot water had taken care of her red ears and nose, but the red rims of her eyes hadn't diminished.

Leslie decided that silence was the best approach, and her patience was rewarded when Sarah suddenly stirred.

"Thank you," she said softly. "I needed . . . someone else to be in charge for a while."

"You don't have to tell me about it, if you don't want to."

"What's to tell? She found the allure of Los

Angeles more potent than mine. I guess I wouldn't feel so bad if I'd seen it coming."

Leslie wanted to tell her that Melissa was a manipulative bimbo, but she caught the words before they spilled out. Sarah might agree, but she would never thank Leslie for being the person who told her so.

"I can't believe it," Leslie said. "You seemed so happy."

"I was. She wanted me to go with her to L.A. She was sure I would go." She chuckled humorlessly. "She was sure I'd go and I was sure she'd stay. What a pair." A gust of wind shook the redwood enclosure and Sarah slid to the lowest seat, up to her chin. "The water — the heat is great. Why are you being so good to me?"

Leslie started to say, "Once a mom, always a mom," but thought better of it. "I'd like to think — even though we got off to a rocky start — that we're friends."

Sarah's lips curved ever so slightly. "Friends," she echoed. Her lower lip quivered and her eyes filled with tears. "Do friends hold you when you're going to cry your eyes out?"

"Yes," Leslie said, feeling tears of sympathy start. She waded from her seat to Sarah's and wrapped Sarah in her arms. "I'm here for you."

Sarah struggled to wake up. Her eyes felt like two cotton balls rolled in gravel. She managed a glance around through tiny slits, and then she remembered where she was. Matt's room.

Her nose twitched. Bacon. Definitely bacon. Her stomach growled. God, she thought, I *am* alive.

She was also naked, a fact she discovered when she got out of bed. She saw a robe on the foot of the bed, then remembered Leslie handing it to her in return for her wet suit. Nothing to be embarrassed about. She put the robe on and then let her nose find the kitchen.

Coffee and bacon. Leslie was forking crispy strips onto paper towels. She glanced up as Sarah came in.

"Welcome to the first day of your vacation," Leslie said. "I took the liberty of calling in for you. For me, too. I didn't have a damn thing worth doing, and cleaning my desk can wait for the new year."

"I didn't leave my desk in the best shape," Sarah said. "I should really take care of a few things —"

"What's the worst thing that can happen if you don't go in today? The mugs are in the cupboard next to the dishwasher."

Sarah found a mug and poured herself what smelled like the perfect cup of French roast. "I guess — well, it'll all be there when I get back from Washington. Just because Richard gave me two weeks off doesn't mean I have to take every single day."

"Yes, it does," Leslie said. "You need to be a little selfish. As your supervisor —"

"Oh, God," Sarah moaned. "I cried all over my boss." She was surprised that she could laugh about it. "I'm sitting in my boss's kitchen, in a robe, scarfing up her coffee, which is excellent by the way."

"I'm sorry I reminded you I'm your boss," Leslie said. "I'm not going to work today either, which makes me officially not your boss at this moment. I hope you like bacon."

"I love it," Sarah said. "I haven't had it for —"

She broke off, and blinked back sudden tears. She hadn't thought more tears were possible.

"Oh, that's right. She was a vegetarian."

Sarah was grateful that Leslie hadn't actually used Melissa's name. "Am I going to be doing this for long?"

"Doing what?"

"Getting teary every time I think about her?"

"Yeah, probably. But you're going to live, and yesterday I wasn't so sure."

"Neither was I. Thanks."

"Don't mention it," Leslie said.

Sarah watched Leslie scramble eggs and told herself she was very lucky. Melissa may have ripped her heart out by the roots, but it could have been worse. She could have been friendless too.

"How would you like to go to Washington for Christmas?" The words were out before Sarah realized she was going to say them.

"I wouldn't want to intrude —"

"You won't. You'll be doing me a big favor. If you'd rather go to Richard's —"

"What do I need to bring?"

Sarah surprised herself by grinning. "Warm clothes. Really warm clothes."

"Okay, I can manage that. I'll go on one condition."

"Which is?"

"I pay my own way —"

"I've already bought the tickets, and they're not refundable, so you're not costing me a thing."

"I can still reimburse you for the ticket."

"It's not necessary," Sarah said firmly.

They locked gazes for a long minute, then Leslie finally said, just as firmly, "I'll buy the groceries."

Sarah sighed with relief. "It's a deal."

The weather gods granted them an on-time flight and clear roads. Leslie could tell nothing of the area surrounding the cabin because it was dark — truly dark. There was no moon, no street lights, and the stars seemed very far away.

"We might have to backtrack to that motel anyway," Sarah was saying. "If we can't get the stove going, or if the electricity is down, it'll be too cold to sleep here without sub-zero sleeping bags."

The ice in the air took Leslie's breath away. "Let's leave the stuff in the four by four, then. Until we're sure."

Sarah was already bounding up the steps to the door. A light came on and Leslie followed more slowly.

"This is great," Sarah called. "The last relative to stay here was my cousin John — he knows how to take care of things. I'll bet he even drained the pipes. I'll go turn the water on." She disappeared into another room, then the back door banged.

Leslie took the opportunity to study the little cabin. The furniture, rugs, curtains — all were unexpectedly clean and in good condition. Some of the tables looked handmade from knotty pine and maple.

The kitchen had a recently purchased refrigerator, and a small microwave on the counter, but the rest was like stepping into a time warp, right down to a squat, wood-burning stove made of cast iron. The counters were tile, but Leslie had never seen a basketweave pattern like it before. And the linoleum — a deep green with white flecks. It took Leslie right back to the first grade.

A note was on the well-scrubbed maple table from cousin John, thanking Sarah for the use of the cabin over Thanksgiving. He added a list of things he thought needed to be done around the place and said he and the kids had cut back the blackberry bushes that had overgrown the gate.

Blackberry bushes. Wouldn't Matt love it here in the summer? Leslie had a fond flashback to the early days of the organic farm she and Richie had run — blackberries so ripe and full · they were like wine, right off the vine. Visions of cobblers and pies danced through her head.

Sarah clumped up the back stairs. "The water is on. Open the taps in here, and I'll take care of the bathroom and the water heater."

After the spluttering died down, Leslie turned the taps off. She lifted the fire cover off the stove and found it ready to light — John was a good guest.

Sarah peeked over Leslie's shoulder. "Great, I'll get the matches. Go check out the bedrooms — take your pick."

The bedrooms were similar, just small rooms with full-sized beds and a wardrobe. The wallpaper looked fairly recent, and Leslie ran a hand over the linen texture, liking the small slivers of wood woven into it. The floors were linoleum of the same antiquity as the kitchen's, but they were obscured by thick Berber rugs in deep forest green. She called, "I'm left-handed, so I'll take the left one, okay?"

"Sure. The stove's going. Let's get the stuff."

Obviously, Sarah loved this place. She was pinging around with more animation than she'd shown on the trip so far.

Another half-hour's labor had them both unpacked, the groceries put away and a fire lit in the living room fireplace to help take the chill off.

They settled in front of the fire with mugs of apple cider heated in the microwave and the last of Melody's mom's gingerbread cookies.

"This place is so you," Leslie said.

"How so?" Sarah nibbled her cookie. Leslie noticed that in firelight, her blue-violet eyes had turned dark purple.

"It's . . . real. I'm feeling like I'm back on the organic farm. It's rare these days a place takes from me instead of me from it. Do you know what I mean?"

Sarah nodded. "This is a far cry from a resort. It takes a lot of work to be comfortable here. My grannie kept it up all by herself for the last thirty years of her life, which is pretty incredible. Well, she had a crew of helpers throughout the summer. Like me, and my cousins. And she stopped chopping her own wood a couple of years before she died."

"She sounds like an amazing woman."

"She was," Sarah said. "She fell in love with an American flyer during World War Two, came to America on the Queen Mary with three thousand other war brides from England and followed my grandfather across the continent, making a home wherever they settled."

Leslie heard the longing in Sarah's voice. "You wish she was here, don't you?"

Sarah's eyes shimmered in the firelight. "She'd have known just what to say, or told me a story about heartbreak leading to triumph, one of her it'll-all-turn-out-in-the-end stories."

They sat in silence for a long while, watching the fire. Leslie found herself nodding off. "I'm going to turn in. I have a feeling morning comes early here."

"It's spectacular," Sarah said with a
"Pleasant dreams."

Leslie glanced back when she reached the door
her room. Sarah was wiping something from he
cheek. "Pleasant dreams to you too," she whispered.

11

Bring me my bow of burning gold
Bring me my arrows of desire.
(William Blake)

Leslie rolled over and sighed deeply into her soft pillow. Her third morning at the farm was starting off just like the first two. The warm bed, utter quiet and gray light urged her to go back to sleep. The electric blanket was humming a lullaby.

The first day it had been after ten before she'd finally managed to stir, but today was Christmas, and she could hear Sarah in the kitchen.

She took a quick shower and rummaged in her suitcase for the comfortable leggings and sweater she'd brought with her. She slipped the gift she'd brought for Sarah into her pocket.

Sarah was dropping spoonfuls of dough ont cookie sheet. She looked up and said, "You miss the sunrise again."

"Merry Christmas to you too."

Sarah's lips curved into the smile Leslie had come to love. "Merry Christmas, sleepyhead."

"It must be the mountain air." Leslie poured herself a cup of coffee and then leaned inquisitively over the bowl of dough. "Scones?"

"Cinnamon scones," Sarah said. "I hope they turn out."

"I'm sure they won't suck."

Sarah shot her a grin. "You're so supportive."

"I try. What can I make?"

"Nothing at all — I've got it covered."

She wandered back to the living room window to see if the landscape had changed. It was highly satisfactory that it had not.

She found every view from every window of the cabin captivating. Snow draped every surface outside, even the rental car. Sarah had obviously been out for a walk — her footprints were the only break in the smooth white powder in front of the house. The footprints disappeared into the trees in the direction of a ridge Sarah said provided the most spectacular view in the area.

The trees were a mix of fir and aspen. The old green firs were flocked with snow. White powder drifted slowly to the ground with each puff of wind. She caught her breath — the sun was coming out for a few moments. Brilliant gold light streamed across the landscape catching the ice-covered limbs of aspen in a radiant display of rainbow colors. Then the sun was gone and the gray light returned, but even that

tinted with the lavender hues of the aspen
ushing against the sky.

"Isn't it amazing when it does that?"

Leslie couldn't believe she hadn't heard or felt
Sarah coming up behind her, not when it seemed her
entire body was attuned to Sarah's every move. "It
still takes my breath away." She reached into her
pocket and turned. "Merry Christmas."

"What's this?" Sarah took the small box. "You
are — so sweet. I didn't get you anything."

"This is something I already had and I think of
you every time I see it — so I think you should have
it."

Sarah opened the box and Leslie was pleased to
see a smile flicker across her face. "I couldn't . . .
could I?"

"You can. It's you."

Sarah lifted the enameled pendant out of the box.
"Where did you get it?"

"It was a gift from Alan. He said that was how
he saw me, but I never thought it was me. But it is
you. She even looks like you."

Sarah went to the mirror over the curio cabinet,
and held the pendant against her sweater. Leslie
compared the lithe figure of Diana drawing her bow
to her mental image of Sarah drawing a bow while
clad only in a skimpy Roman toga. She was still
blushing when she realized Sarah was staring at her
in the mirror.

"What can I say? Thank you."

"You don't think it's tacky that I gave you
something my ex-husband gave me?"

"Not at all — it's lovely. Wasn't Diana pure of
heart?"

"She was. Chaste, beautiful and deadly to any
who offended her."

Sarah slipped the thin black cord over her and let the pendant settle onto her chest. "A, deadly?" Only to my composure, Leslie thoug Before she could answer, Sarah went on, "Of cours I'm chaste now, and I probably will be forever."

Leslie rolled her eyes before she could stop herself, but to her relief Sarah laughed. "I'm wallowing, I know," she said.

"I wasn't going to say anything." Leslie glanced out the window, eager to get Sarah's gaze off her red cheeks.

The oven timer buzzed and Sarah hurried into the kitchen. "Scones are done," she called after a moment. "Time for breakfast."

The scones were delectable with butter and jam, and eggs with Tabasco and cheese gave Leslie the energy to suggest a foray into the garden to fix the gate. She plodded after Sarah, who bounded up the slope like a snow gazelle.

"How come you're not breathing hard?" Leslie helped knock snow off the gate, which hung from one hinge.

"It's not because I'm in great shape or anything." Sarah examined the fence post, then pulled a hammer out of her pocket. "The nails have just pulled out. Probably need a new post — this one's looking pretty rickety." She hammered the hinge back into place while Leslie held the gate in position.

"You really love it here, don't you?"

"Every inch. I'm glad I came — thank you for coming with me. I might not have, left to my own devices." She stepped back to examine her handiwork. "This may not hold, but there's not much to be done about it until spring."

"Hey, I'm just avoiding Grateful Dead memory week."

arah gave her a look that stopped Leslie's heart. aid, "Don't give me that, you're here for other asons."

Leslie wondered in a panic just how much Sarah suspected. Then she told herself to calm down. "Okay, I'm here because I wanted to get away from my life for a while, and help you get away from yours."

"That's better." Sarah's smile was wry. "Let's at least be honest with each other, okay?"

"Deal." Leslie mimed spitting on her glove and held out her hand. Sarah giggled, copied the motion and they shook on it.

Sarah popped the lid on the sparkling cider and filled both mugs. "Sorry about the lack of crystal — and champagne."

Leslie clinked her mug to Sarah's. "Happy new year."

"To auld lang syne." Sarah noticed Leslie drank as thirstily as she did. The snow shoveling earlier in the day had left them both exhausted and drained. Even steak and potatoes hadn't refilled Sarah's tank. The cider tasted like nectar.

"I don't think I'm going to make it to midnight." Leslie stretched out on the sofa. "I'm not used to all this activity."

"Last New Year's Eve I went to bed at nine," Sarah said. She had thought this year would be so very different. "I'm going to do better this year. But I don't know by how much."

Leslie yawned. "Sorry. I'm kinda glad we don't have champagne — the air here is rarefied enough."

"It's a good vintage." Sarah inhaled deeply. could almost feel the air scrubbing her lungs fre urban grime. "Fruity, mellow, with a buttery unc taste."

Leslie mumbled a response and then was silent. Leslie's breathing deepened as Sarah gently spread an afghan over her. She stood looking down at Leslie for a few minutes, realizing she had never studied her face.

For instance, she had never noticed that Leslie's nose had a small bump at the top, and her eyebrows were not as black as her hair. She knew the eyes behind the peach-tinted lids were deep brown, ringed with yellow, but hadn't realized that her lower lip was slightly more red than the upper — at least it looked that way in the firelight. How had she ever thought Leslie cold?

She retired to the big, soft chair closer to the fire and reached for *Pride and Prejudice*. She was approaching the final chapters, with the happy ending just in the offing. She opened to her bookmark, but didn't begin reading. Instead, she wondered what Melissa was doing.

Pressing the flesh with anybody who's anybody and telling them about her novels and screenplays and grants, no doubt. Would Melissa tell anyone she had a broken heart? Maybe, and she'd believe it was true, even if it wasn't.

She asked the fire if her heart was broken, but received only a soothing crackling in response. Something was broken — if not her heart, then something near enough to make the distinction moot.

New Year's Resolution: No more Romance. She wrote it on her mental notepad in big letters. Resolution number two: No more thinking about Melissa.

ne resolutely turned her attention to her book finished with a pleased sigh. As she set it aside, slie turned on her side and said, "Dorfing snees."

It was two minutes to midnight, and Sarah decided Leslie shouldn't miss the coming of the New Year. She gently shook her. "Hey, it's almost midnight."

"Umm, goody."

"Wake up — it's almost midnight."

Leslie's eyes opened and Sarah was caught off-guard by the softness of her smile as she focused. "Couldn't let me miss it, huh?"

"Nope."

Just as Leslie sat up the mantel clock began to chime the hour. "Happy New Year again," she said. Her hair was tousled even more wildly than usual.

Sarah was seized by an overwhelming need. She sat down on the sofa next to Leslie. "Can I ask you a favor?"

"You can always ask," Leslie said. She flicked her gaze to the fire.

"Would you hold me? I feel lonely all of a sudden."

Leslie's answer was to tuck the afghan around Sarah's shoulders, then pull Sarah gently against her. "That better?"

"Much." She watched the flames leap behind the isinglass for a few minutes, then stirred. "I'm sorry to be so needy all the time."

"We all have our moments," Leslie said, in a low voice.

"Will you let me know when you have yours? I owe you."

Leslie cleared her throat. "You'll be the first to know."

When Sarah woke she couldn't move her neck.

She groaned and struggled to sit up, only to disc[...]
she was using Leslie's thigh as a pillow.

Leslie made a sound similar to Sarah's groan.
"My leg is asleep."

"I think my neck is broken."

"God, it's hard getting old."

"We're not old. We're middle-aged."

"Know what the definition of middle age is? When
you think you'll feel better tomorrow."

Sarah laughed and her neck began to loosen up.
Leslie gritted her teeth when Sarah brushed against
her leg. "Does that tickle?"

"Don't you dare," Leslie said. "I'm letting it wake
up slowly."

"It's better if you get it over fast." She reached
for Leslie's thigh.

"Oh, you bitch," Leslie gasped as she tried to
knock away Sarah's hands. Sarah knew perfectly well
that every motion was making Leslie's leg tingle even
more.

"I'm only trying to help."

"Liar!" Leslie managed to drag herself to the end
of the sofa. "You're so cruel."

"Let me make it up to you." Sarah leaned toward
Leslie with her most innocent expression. Then she
seized Leslie's thigh and shook it as hard as she
could.

Leslie responded with a shriek. Sarah laughed
helplessly as Leslie pummeled her with a pillow.

"Truce," she finally yelled.

Leslie delivered a few more blows, then subsided.
"You're a sadist," she said with a pout.

"I try." Sarah stood up. "Three a.m. on New
Year's Day. I think I'll get some more shut eye."

"That sounds like an excellent idea."

Sarah paused at her bedroom door. "Les?"

Leslie turned.

Sarah took the two steps necessary to press her lips briefly to Leslie's. "First kiss of the new year. Thank you."

Leslie returned the light kiss with one of her own. "You're welcome."

"If Matt weren't coming home, I don't think I could leave," Leslie told Sarah. She rinsed the last dish and set it in the drainer.

Sarah whacked the stove flue one last time and a cloud of black soot burst from the front of the stove. "I know what you mean. I've made a promise to myself to come here at least twice a year. I can only leave so much up to other people."

"Will you be back during blackberry season?"

"That's a good time of the year to be here. Zucchini comes in right around then — lasagna, zucchini bread, blackberry cobbler."

"Yum," Leslie said. "You have soot all over your forehead."

Sarah's voice was muffled from inside the oven. "If it's only on my forehead I'm doing great. I don't think this has been cleaned since my grandmother died."

"I'm going to finish packing." Leslie started to leave the kitchen, but something made her pause. Sarah looked pretty damned adorable with her head in the oven, and . . . well, there was just nothing else to be done. She slipped over to the back door and scooped a handful of snow off the porch rail.

Who would have thought that the oven would amplify a screech like that, Leslie thought as she bolted out the front door. She took the path toward

224

the garden and wished she'd had the foresight to put her coat on before she plopped the handful of snow into the waistband of Sarah's jeans.

Her headlong flight ended when a large, wet snowball hit her on the back, instantly soaking through her sweater. If flight wouldn't work, then she had no choice but to defend herself.

She quickly discovered that Sarah's aim was better than hers. "I give, I give — you win." She put her hands in the air like a captured desperado.

Sarah advanced slowly, a snowball in one reddened hand. "I do believe that I would like to see your belly button."

"You wouldn't," Leslie said, appalled. Under other circumstances she'd happily show Sarah her belly button.

"Take your punishment now, or spend the rest of your life wondering when it'll come." Sarah packed a little more dripping snow onto the snowball. "Belly button, please."

Leslie reluctantly raised the hem of her sweater, then pulled the front of her jeans down just enough. She gritted her teeth. "Do your worst, you fiend."

The freezing snowball on her warm belly knocked the breath out of her. Sarah pulled the sweater down over the snowball and patted it. Already, water was running down into Leslie's slacks.

"We're going to miss our plane if you keep fooling around," Sarah said. She turned and walked toward the cabin.

Leslie dug the snow out from under her sweater and formed a nice, compact snowball with it. She looked at Sarah's back.

"I wouldn't do that if I were you," Sarah said, without even looking back.

She's asking for it, Leslie thought. She held back

for as long as she could but couldn't stop the impulse.

Sarah glanced over her shoulder just in time, then ducked. The snowball flew through the open front door.

"Shit," Leslie said. She hurried inside to see if she'd broken anything. There was a wet splotch on the glass-doored knick-knack cabinet just inside the door, but fortunately nothing was broken. "I'll get some paper towels," she told Sarah. "It seemed like a good idea at the time."

Sarah laughed and went back to scraping ash out of the oven. Leslie mopped the floor then dried the glass doors. What she had thought was frosting on the glass turned out to be ordinary dust, and she ended up wiping down the entire front.

She had just finished the job to her satisfaction when she realized what she was looking at through the glass. A picture of Sarah and several other people standing next to Ronald Reagan, at the White House. She blinked, then opened the door to examine everything more closely. Then she realized the cupboard was devoted to Sarah's archery career. There were pictures of her with trophies, numerous certificates and plaques, and several arrows with tags. She picked one up — it was heavier than it looked. The tag read, "Seoul, 1988."

As she put the arrow back in its place, she dislodged a jeweler's box and it fell to the floor, spilling its contents on the soft rug.

Leslie's heart stopped for a moment. My God, was that what she thought it was? Three medals, one bronze, two gold. The bronze was engraved "XX Olympiad, Los Angeles." The front was the Olympic seal. The back was the classic figure of a Greek archer. The two gold medals were from Seoul, one with a single archer, and the second with three archers.

"Are you going to spend all day — oh."

Leslie looked up. "You really know how to hide your light under a bushel, don't you?"

Sarah was blushing. "I — did you ever see *Catch-22?*"

"Yeah, it was required viewing for aspiring flower children. So?"

"Yossarian says that Olympic medals and tennis trophies just signified that the owner had done something of no benefit to anyone at all more capably than everyone else at that moment in time. I had a girlfriend who always introduced me as the Olympic gold medalist, and sometimes she omitted my name altogether." She knelt next to Leslie and took one of the gold medals. "They helped me get into law school, and I know I got my interview at CompuSoft because I was still putting it on my résumé — and the interviewer asked about my experiences. I needed to . . . get some distance."

"So you just leave them here on a shelf?" Leslie thought that she would have had the medals in a safe deposit box and the photos on her wall for the world to see.

"Actually, I'm going to take the medals back with me. I think I've finally outgrown the shadow they cast." Sarah ran a fingertip lightly over the engraving. "And a little self-esteem boost wouldn't hurt right now." She tucked the medals back in the jeweler's box and got to her feet. "And we're going to miss our plane if we're not out of here by two."

Leslie closed the cabinet doors and peered at the picture of Sarah at the White House. She looked so young, and so happy. She must have been amazing to know, Leslie thought.

She laughed to herself when she remembered blaming Richard for her crush on Sarah. She had behaved very badly from the outset and, in a way, didn't deserve the deepening love she felt. It was an hourly torture to be so close to her every day, but an exquisite torture she would miss. She would miss Sarah's laughter and wit even more. Seeing her just at work wouldn't be enough.

Love was not an unknown quantity to her. She knew that she was capable of love — she loved Matt fiercely, and Richard deeply. And she'd loved Alan, much as she might have loved a brother if she'd had one. What she felt for Sarah sprang from the same place — it was strong and enduring. But her love for Sarah was entwined with desire and passion, a complex combination she had never experienced before.

Did she dare hope that some day — soon, please — Sarah would return these feelings? She tried not to read too much into Sarah's new year's kiss, or the easy way Sarah took her hand when they were out walking to hurry her up. It was obvious Sarah was comfortable with her, too comfortable to have nary a sexual thought. Leslie knew she had Sarah's respect and genuine affection. If only, she thought. If only she could have more.

Melody greeted Sarah with an I-told-you-so look. "Did I say this weekend would be clear and warm? It's spring!"

"Finally," Sarah said. "I thought it would never stop raining. It was getting —" She let out a squawk as something hit her in the back.

"You left your mitt at my house again," Leslie said from her office door.

Sarah picked up her mitt and then stuck her tongue out at Leslie. "Stop inviting me for pity dinners after softball, then."

"If I did that you'd starve." Leslie disappeared into her office.

Sarah turned to Melody. "She always has to have the last word, doesn't she?"

"You just figured that out?" Melody's look said Sarah was slow on the uptake. "She's the Queen of the Last Word."

Leslie's voice floated out to them. "Am not."

Sarah shared a laugh with Melody. "She can be so irritating."

"And you love it," Melody said, then she turned to answer her phone.

Sarah settled in at her desk, but found Melody's last words running through her head. Do I love it, she asked herself. Certainly she was very fond of Leslie — she was more than a work friend. They had joined a women's softball team together and indulged in their mutual love of bad science fiction movies — something they both shared with Matt. Matt had taught Sarah to inline skate, and she had promised to teach him how to shoot a bow. Leslie was helping her shop for a house down on the peninsula, but that was because she knew the lay of the land. There wasn't any more to it, she told herself firmly. Leslie's just a generous person.

She recalled her New Year's Resolutions. Not thinking about Melissa had been easier than expected. Not thinking about Romance — she had been doing very well with that one, until lately. She sternly reminded herself that she didn't believe in Romance anymore. Melody was a master of innuendo and that was all.

When she got home that night she found she couldn't shake Melody's phrase. "And you love it," she'd said. Love Leslie? She told herself to be honest and admit it — she did love Leslie, loved her like a sister.

She made herself a quick stir fry for dinner, then she went for a long walk. There hadn't been any fog for more than a week, and the daylight was getting a little longer. She strolled the length of the Castro merchant district, dodging what seemed like an endless parade of couples holding hands.

The Castro Theatre was showing *Desert Hearts* but Sarah was hardly going to watch it again — at least not in this millennium. She would miss the bustle of the area if she moved, but not so much that a quiet house in the Mountain View area didn't appeal. Her roots were sinking into MagicWorks, into Richard's kindness and the programmers' playfulness. Hanging out with Leslie had allowed her to get to know the San Jose area better. She'd like a place similar to Leslie's — a big kitchen, enough yard for a hot tub, and a hilltop view of something more than rows of houses.

She turned into an alley to cut over to Noe and startled two young women in ardent embrace. She went quickly by them, trying and failing to ignore the half-bared breasts and lips bruised with kisses. She was discomfited by a sudden mental image of Leslie in the hot tub.

Don't go there, she warned herself. She quickened her pace, but the steep uphill on Noe forced her to slow down, and she found herself admitting she couldn't outrun the silly idea Melody had planted in her head.

It was silly, she told herself later that night. She turned out the light and commanded herself to sleep, but instead she remembered watching Leslie dance with that woman at the Nestle party. She wondered what it would be like to dance with Leslie. But if she asked Leslie out dancing it would be like . . . like a date. They were buddies. Buddies don't date.

She wrapped her arms around her pillow and tried to sleep. She slipped into a light doze and rubbed her cheek against the pillow as if it were Leslie's. Her entire body felt warm and heavy and her mouth ached to open against Leslie's, to taste her and breathe her in.

When she awoke in the morning she knew she had been dreaming. And she knew the identity of the voluptuous dream woman with the wild black curls.

"Wiggle your fingers, your arm is too stiff." Sarah tipped Matt's head slightly more to the left. "Do you see the gold? Do you see the line between the tip of your arrow and the gold?"

"Yes," Matt said. He wiggled his fingers, then released the arrow. His bow rocked forward in his hand after the arrow left it, then he let out a whoop. "Bulls-eye! I finally got a bulls-eye!"

Sarah congratulated him, then said, "Archery isn't football, you don't get to do a special dance during competition."

"I know," he said. "But I was starting to think I'd never make it." He nocked his next arrow and Sarah stood back to watch his form.

She'd been giving him lessons for two months now, and he was improving rapidly. She glanced over her shoulder at Leslie, not surprised to find Leslie's gaze on her. She hadn't been surprised at that for some time, and she'd come to expect the caress she found in Leslie's eyes. She'd resisted believing in it at first, but she believed now.

"Finish shooting your quiver," she told Matt. "I won't give you any pointers and we'll see how you do. Just remember, there's no need to hurry. Sight the target. Focus on the line —"

"And let fly, I know," he said.

Sarah joined Leslie on the bench. "He's getting much better."

"It's nice to see him stick with something," Leslie said. "You're a great influence. I'm sure it's the first thing he'll tell his Dad when he gets off the plane tomorrow."

"Hey, it's been a pretty good day, all in all."

"That it has," Leslie said, watching Matt. "The guy from Disney was practically panting, wasn't he, though he wasn't at all the corporate fascist I had expected."

Sarah laughed, and Leslie turned to look at her inquiringly. "You and your preconceived notions."

Leslie rolled her eyes, but she was smiling.

"So do you think I should buy the house?"

"It's a great deal. I'm sure it'll be a good investment."

"A house is more than an investment," Sarah said. Her heart was racing. "It's the people in it. It's too big for me to fill up by myself." She couldn't look at Leslie. "I'd need help."

She put her arm on the back of the bench and, after a moment, Leslie mirrored her pose. Sarah's little finger brushed against Leslie's, sending an acute tingling down her arm.

Leslie's little finger brushed back, and Sarah let

her gaze lock with Leslie's as their fingers hooked together.

Leslie said in a low voice, "Maybe you should hold off on the house for a while."

"Maybe I should. Things change. People change."

Leslie looked down at their linked fingers. "Hearts heal. And surprise you."

Tears sprang into Sarah's eyes. "This feels comfortable." She squeezed Leslie's little finger with her own.

"To me, too," Leslie said. She swallowed noisily, then repeated, "To me, too."

They shared a similar smile, and Sarah's heart settled into a calm, easy rhythm. How surprising, she thought. This love wasn't a tidal wave so much as the tide finally coming to the longed-for shore. It poured into every part of her body and soul, washing away any fears still lingering, and leaving no room for doubts to creep in. She studied the promise in Leslie's eyes and anticipated the passion offered in her parted-lip smile.

Sarah looked her fill at the curves of Leslie's face. When Matt hollered again that he had hit the bulls-eye, Sarah knew he was not the only one.

Epigraph Sources

1 She had been forced into prudence in her youth, she learned romance as she grew older. (Jane Austen, *Persuasion*)

2 Life itself is but motion, and can never be without desire... (Thomas Hobbes, *Leviathan*, Pt. 1, Chapter 6)

3 A time to embrace.... (Ecclesiastes 3:6)

4 Desire is moved with violent motion...and is called love. (Socrates, quoted in Plato, *Phaedrus*)

5 Your embraces alone give life to my heart. (Author unknown, *Love Songs of the New Kingdom*)

6 To love oneself is the beginning of a life-long romance. (Oscar Wilde, *Phrases and Philosophies for the Use of the Young*)

7 The moments of the past do not remain still; they retain in our memory the motion which drew them towards the future, towards a future which has itself become the past... (Marcel Proust, *Remembrance of Things Past*, Volume 11)

8 ...Motion is a harmony, and dance Magnificent. (William Wordsworth, *Home at Grasmere*)

9 You desire to embrace it, to caress it, to possess it... (Henry James, *Italian Hours*, Section 2)

10 An arrow for the heart like a sweet voice. (Lord Byron, "Dedication," *Don Juan*,/Canto XV)

11 Bring me my bow of burning gold
Bring me my arrows of desire. (William Blake, *Milton*)

About the Author

Karin Kallmaker was born in 1960 and raised by her loving, middle-class parents in California's Central Valley. The physician's Statement of Live Birth plainly declares, "Sex- Female" and "Cry: Lusty." Both are still true.

From a normal childhood and equally unremarkable public school adolescence, she went on to obtain an ordinary Bachelor's degree from the California State University at Sacramento. At the age of 16, eyes wide open, she fell into the arms of her first and only sweetheart.

Ten years later, after seeing the film *Desert Hearts*, her sweetheart descended on the Berkeley Public Library determined to find some of "those" books. "Rule, Jane" led to "Lesbianism - Fiction" and then on to book after self-affirming book by and about lesbians. These books were the encouragement Karin needed to forget the so-called "mainstream" and spin her first romance for lesbians. That manuscript became her first novel, *In Every Port*. She now lives in the San Francisco Bay Area with that very same sweetheart; she is a one woman woman. The happily-ever-after couple became Mom and Moogie to Kelson in 1995 and Eleanor in 1997. They celebrate their twenty-seventh anniversary in 2004.

Karin also writes as Laura Adams, her science fiction and fantasy persona.

Publications from
BELLA BOOKS, INC.
The best in contemporary lesbian fiction

P.O. Box 10543, Tallahassee, FL 32302
Phone: 800-729-4992
www.bellabooks.com

IN EVERY PORT by Karin Kallmaker. 224 pp. Jessica's sexy,
adventuresome travels.   ISBN 1-931513-36-8 $12.95

TOUCHWOOD by Karin Kallmaker. 240 pp. Loving
May/December romance.   ISBN 1-931513-37-6 $12.95

WATERMARK by Karin Kallmaker. 248 pp. One burning
question . . . how to lead her back to love? ISBN 1-931513-38-4 $12.95

EMBRACE IN MOTION by Karin Kallmaker. 240 pp. A
whirlwind love affair.   ISBN 1-931513-39-2 $12.95

ONE DEGREE OF SEPARATION by Karin Kallmaker. 232 pp.
Can an Iowa City librarian find love and passion when a California
girl surfs into the close-knit Dyke Capital of the Midwest?
                                          ISBN 1-931513-30-9 $12.95

CRY HAVOC A Detective Franco Mystery by Baxter Clare. 240 pp.
A dead hustler with a headless rooster in his lap sends Lt. L.A.
Franco headfirst against Mother Love.   ISBN 1-931513931-7 $12.95

DISTANT THUNDER by Peggy J. Herring. 294 pp. Bankrobbing
drifter Cordy awakens strange new feelings in Leo in this romantic
tale set in the old West.   ISBN 1-931513-28-7 $12.95

COP OUT by Claire McNab. 216 pp. 4th Detective Inspector
Carol Ashton Mystery.   ISBN 1-931513-29-5 $12.95

BLOOD LINK by Claire McNab. 159 pp. 15th Detective
Inspector Carol Ashton Mystery. Is Carol unwittingly playing
into a deadly plan?   ISBN 1-931513-27-9 $12.95

TALK OF THE TOWN by Saxon Bennett. 239 pp.
With enough beer, barbecue and B.S., anything
is possible!   ISBN 1-931513-18-X $12.95